The Sky After Rain

ฟ้าหลังฝน

THE SKY AFTER RAIN

a Novel

by

D. E. LEE

BRIGHT
HORSE
BOOKS

Brighthorse Books
13202 N River Drive
Omaha, NE 68112
brighthorsebooks.com

ISBN: 978-1-944467-03-6

Cover Photo © imagedepotpro
Author Photo: Linda Olsen

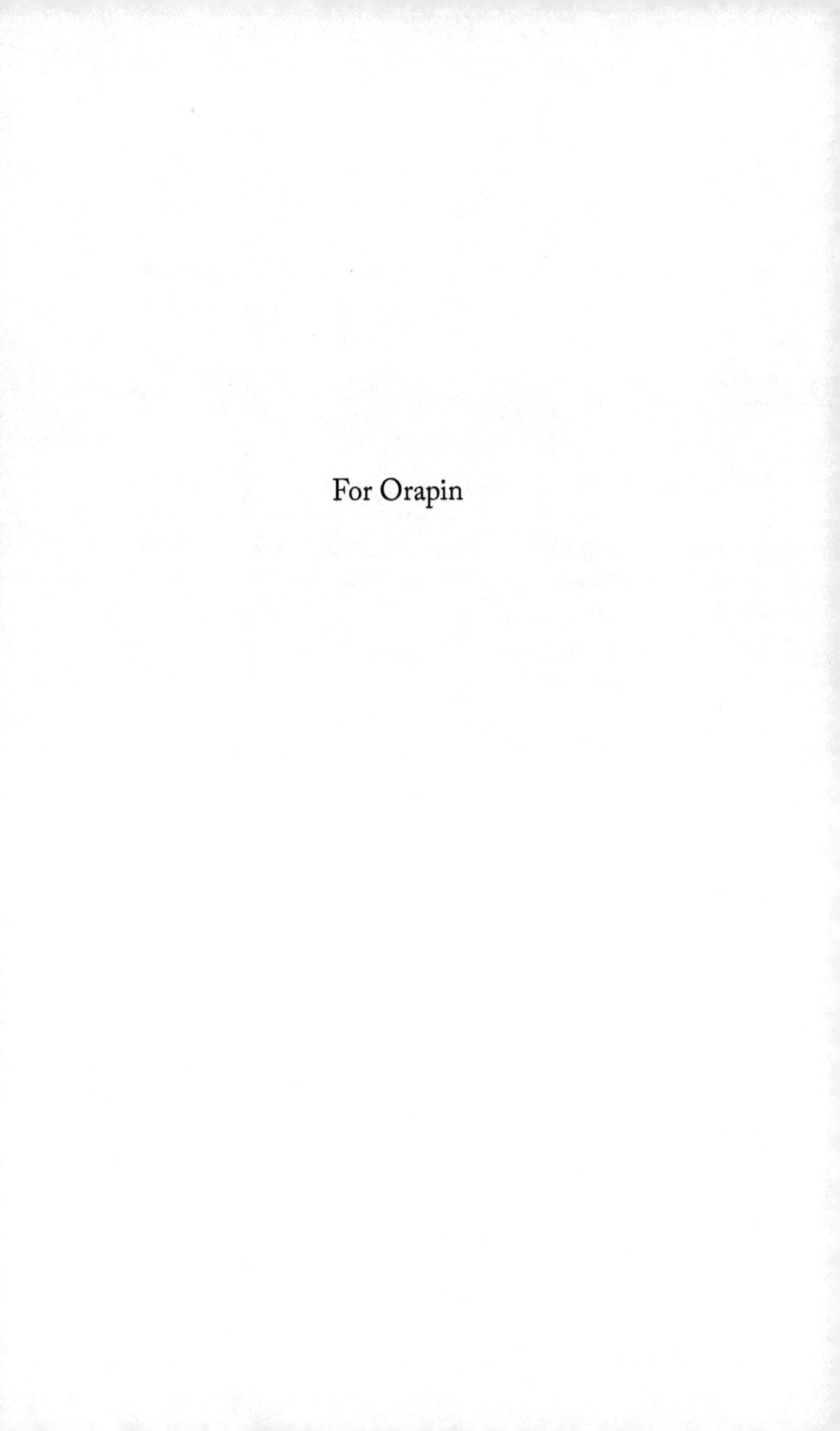

For Orapin

The Sky After Rain

ฟ้าหลังฝน

"Where there is danger some salvation grows there, too"
Friedrich Hölderlin—"Patmos"

Amnaj Boonngamanong

THERE WAS A RUN on plywood. Amnaj pushed out from the dark gloom of En La Playa into the sharp bright light of morning. Jimmy Nails waited on an overturned cable spool by the truck. His hands glinting in the sunlight. Amnaj strode toward Nails.

Plywood would go fast. And bottled water and batteries and generators. The girls could get water and batteries. He had two generators and several gas cans stored beneath shelves of vodka and rum. The generators sat idle inside yellow exoskeletons. Oiled and lean, they waited like bored dogs in the shade of the storage room.

He smelled the dust from the crushed shells of the parking lot and looked past Jimmy Nails at the dunes, then beyond the dunes at the Gulf of Mexico. Flat as glass, green as mouthwash. Green and anemic as the Suzuki Swift pulling into the parking lot.

Nails jumped down from the spool. Beefy brow, shoulders like hams. Nails had the hard knock looks of a bowling pin. He was there. Simple and slow. His skin, sweating in the sun, a map of the hard road he'd been down. Dark, hard eyes that shunned light, that seemed to be on the verge of death. But he was there. He was ready.

Then Nokyung drove up. Here's a good girl, for what it's worth, Amnaj thought. Satisfied, complacent. He tried to convince her to get a nicer car. She wanted the Swift. It's practical, she'd said. It's cheap, she'd said. That's the problem, he told her. It won't get you what you need. And what do I need? *A good girl, and always a challenge.*

Her legs swung out. Feet on the shell pavement. *Such energy.* Now trotting—*always on the run.* She pressed her hands together and bowed. Straight to the point. The plain face impervious to the elements, to the snaps and jabs of her plain life. But she jumped to it. Whatever was asked of her.

Wasting your time here, he thought, watching her. *Plain with no chance. But a good girl.*

Then about the plywood. Broad, flat sheets and a box of sixpenny nails. Get it before it's gone.

Nokyung looked eager.

Nails was there, ready.

For a moment, as if there were no hurry, they stood gazing over the flat and placid water, the green surface of the Gulf, the cloudless blue sky dripping into the horizon. And beyond that, beyond what they could see, a raging and powerful storm none of them could imagine.

"Where's your sister?" Amnaj spoke to Nokyung. He spoke in Thai. Their language excluded and insulated. *No one else's business.* Jimmy Nails looked indifferent, still staring at the water as if he expected something might wash ashore. It was hard to read that man. He seemed to hold a treasure from a child's imagination in his mind.

Nokyung shrugged. "Getting a husband," she said. "That's what we're here for, isn't it?"

"She should be here to help out."

The heat of the morning warmed the skin.

"Finding a husband," Nokyung said. "That's what you wanted, wasn't it?"

He tossed the key. "Jimmy, get the windows down." He turned to Nokyung. "Find a husband, yes. Find a husband. Not sleep with every man in town. Know what they call her? Hasn't she got any sense?"

"Maybe you can ask her."

He rested his arms on the truck rails and stared through the cab at the coarse hair on the back of Jimmy Nails's head. Hard to read, unmoving, content, it seemed, to sit there all day. And beyond, the calm water.

He shook his head. "And how many days left?"

Nokyung blinked, as if startled. "Days? Our visas lapsed weeks ago." She lifted a foot from a flip-flop and scratched the back of her leg.

Plain, he thought, *but graceful.*

"Uncle, I want to go home. I hate it here. I hate the bar. I hate farang."

Amnaj exhaled. "Huh . . . you might as well stay. Make some money."

Shielding her eyes from the sun. "How will I do that? I send my money to my mother. Jit says I can work at the dry cleaners. Maybe I can save."

"You work in the bar."

"I *hate* the bar."

"It's because you don't treat the customers—"

"Like Joom? Like Boom Boom Joom? You want me to do that?"

He pursed his lips. She was angry, though who could guess?

A pinch in her lips, a squint in her eye. Angry and subtle and calm and flat like the Gulf waters. A murmur of anger beneath. *Plain*, he thought, *and hopeless*. Twenty-seven and never a man. *A hopeless girl*. "You shouldn't have come," he said. "If you didn't want to. What are you doing here?"

"You made it out so good, Uncle. You filled Joom with hope and got Ma excited, too. They said, 'Go, go,' and what could I do? You made it out so good. Not like this."

He was tired, and there was a run on plywood, but he couldn't let it go. "You don't try, ลูก. Do you have a date? Do you meet a man?"

Angry, subtle, calm, flat, a good girl, he thought, *and plain and hopeless*.

He noticed her calves tightening, her foot wanting to stomp. "Yes," she said. "I have dates, and I hate farang. So, no more. I want to go home."

He was tired, and she was hopeless, and there was a run on plywood. He waved her off. "Go cut fruit for tonight and clean up."

Nokyung bowed. She trotted across the parking lot. She stopped under the large, bent sign above the door and called out. She pointed up at the sign, at the bone-white words *En La Playa*. "Your sign is bent and this is a stupid name! You are Thai, not Mexican!" He waved her off. A gust of wind behind her, she went inside.

He slid into the cab next to Jimmy Nails who was slowly scraping his hooks together as if to sharpen them. *Poor bastard. Why'd he settle for those old things, like torture devices out of a horror movie?* Get something that resembled hands. But he didn't seem to mind. He did all right. Cleaned out the Mexican's roofer money at the pool table. Didn't seem to mind that, either.

He turned the key. A blast of cool air shot from the vents. He'd forgotten his wallet. "Be right back." He opened the door. He strode across the lot. *So, the sign was bent.* Seventeen years ago he'd arrived in Midsummer, Florida, with his American wife and put up that sign. *So, it was bent.* A little joke inspired by an influx of Mexicans to the Panhandle. *Seventeen years.* They'd done pretty well. A touch of paint from time to time. They'd weathered the storms, and the sign was bent. *So what?* And Katia had come along after his American wife lost interest in the business. And Katia found Maria, and with his nieces, all of them dark and delicious under the track lights, they looked Mexican, and who really noticed anyway? He'd never closed. *Seventeen years.* And he'd never closed the doors. Not a single day. So, the name was Mexican. What was her point? So, the sign was bent, *so what?*

Inside the light was green coming through a painted window. A mounted television flickered red and blue. Cool air tightened his skin. A glow behind the counter and the sound of dull knocking on wood. He passed a table with bedding piled neatly on it and went around the corner. Nokyung was crouched on the floor like an upcountry girl over a chopping board with baskets of limes and oranges and lemons at her feet. She sliced through the rinds quickly, collecting the pieces with a swift motion and piling them in containers. *Plain,* and nimble with a knife. Both girls were. His sister, Manee, their mother, the best cook in Mae Ai, had taught them well.

When he bought a pig for the grill, the girls attacked it like tigers. Every joint severed by the sharp and shiny knives, every bone picked clean of meat, nothing to waste. He found his wallet and made a noise to break her concentration.

"You have a room upstairs," she said without looking up. "Why don't you sleep there?"

He glanced at the bedding on the table. "I get my rest," he said.

"Katia can close up," she said. "You added that small apartment, and you don't use it."

An orange fanned open. A fine citrus fragrance sprayed upward.

"What do you care where I sleep?"

She sliced through a lemon. Metal clacked the wood, clacked with irritation. She wouldn't say a thing, not in anger, her face hidden by a long shadow of hair. Like her mother, she could throw off a thorny emotion with piercing accuracy. Round in the face like her mother, his poor sister, and plain and hopeless, just like Manee—with graceful, long fingers, and good.

He glanced at the television. A hurricane named Molly had whirled between Haiti and Cuba and was scraping the thumb of the Yucatan. A reporter in a yellow raincoat shouted wet-faced into a microphone. Video of a man with all his belongings in a black plastic sack being blown up and down a palm-lined street. The dark red center of the storm like a puncture wound. The path projected into the Gulf then broadened from Brownsville to Apalachicola Bay. Midsummer smack in the middle.

He walked to the truck. Jimmy Nails was sweating, a bare

arm hanging outside the window. Inside, Amnaj gazed over the calm, green water. *You'd never guess what was out there.* He thought of the plywood ramparts defending En La Playa against the storm.

Nokyung Janpong

A YACHT WENT MISSING in the Gulf. A family of five, the report said. The sister of one of the missing said they hadn't had the boat very long. Her eyes were red, her hair whiplashed by wind near Tampa. A blade of white light struck Nokyung's eye. She turned from the television bolted at an angle in the corner. Seeing Castro, she reached into the cooler. She served what they wanted. What she wouldn't do was smile. Not even for Castro, a decent enough man, who carried a notebook pinched between his fingers. He smiled often, though it was a lazy smile, one that never committed to anything. He'd once told her he was the kind of man more interested in how many angels could dance on the head of a pin than what a pin was good for. She'd told him a pin had many uses and named several. He'd laughed at each suggestion and held his hand across his chest, patting it as if holding a baby, and said, when she had finished, "Charmed. Completely." She set the Corona and cup of ice up on the bar. He opened the notebook and began writing.

Nokyung scanned the bar. Katia at the end of the counter with SevenEight. She looked wilted and handed him money. She was always doing that. And then he would hand over some of it to Amnaj. SevenEight's voice rose in anger over the sound of the television. Nokyung glared at Amnaj.

"He brings customers," he'd said once when she complained.

"He makes her a whore," she said now.

His indulgent smile irritated her.

"Is this your bar?" he said. "Are you running it now? Serve the drinks, and do as you're told. She doesn't mind, so why is it your business?"

Nokyung went away silent and perplexed. It was true. Katia never complained.

The afternoons were all right. Before the lights dimmed. When Castro came and perched on a stool in the corner. The green light through the painted window invited an aquatic feel. She liked how Castro's face lit up with some strange idea. When he clicked his pen suddenly and attacked the page. She remembered Maria asking if he was writing a book. He'd shaken his head. Taking notes on us? she asked. Nope, he said. Not even. It's like being at the small town version of the UN or the IHOP, he told her, with emphasis on the international. And when she looked puzzled, he continued. Your Spanish, their Thai. He glanced at SevenEight. I don't know what he speaks. But it's a delight. A symphony of humanity. Maria looked puzzled. She laughed and said, You are kidding me, right? Yes, he said. I'm kidding you. Now go away.

So, no one knew, and Nokyung never felt curious. She wiped the counter before he arrived, made it clean, and prepared his drink. Always the same. Corona and a cup of ice. She watched him squeeze the lime over the ice and pour slowly, as if fascinated by the way the thin yellow liquid wandered downward over the ice. Sips here and there. Mostly, he looked around, clicked his pen, and wrote. In the afternoons, the music was low, and Castro was pleasant, rarely initiating conversation but always willing to set the pen down between the pages and talk. An easy, lazy smile, one without commitment, and smart words—they knew he was awfully smart—and a gentle, forgiving laugh.

Amnaj balanced his hand on Maria's shoulder and turned up the volume on the television. Katia looked up, a waterfall of light cascading down her face. Shots of choppy sea, of cutters churning up froth, of helicopters splashing through rain. Debris on the water bobbed helplessly, and bodies plucked up like clothes from the wash. Nokyung felt herself drifting, squinting into the ambiguous light of the bar. Joom, under a reddish track light, arranged spicy beef on a platter at the buffet table. Younger and fearless, her eyes splashed with a spirited light.

An abrupt sound, an angry bark. "Serves them right!"

Everyone but SevenEight turned to see Nails chalking his cue. SevenEight stared at the television and tipped back a bottle of beer. Nails set the chalk down on the head rail. "Bunch of fools," Nails said, turning away. "Why I keep my nigger ass on land." He lined up the shot.

Katia rapped the counter. "Maria, get ice."

Maria looked embarrassed. SevenEight stood up. Water dripped, bottle to counter.

Amnaj turned, a needled face as if accused. "What's with you?"

"Don't stand there." Katia glared at Maria. "Get it now."

Maria scurried off. Joom, behind her, stared at the television.

SevenEight touched Katia's hair. She flinched. He smiled and jumped off the stool. "Later," he said.

Nails banked the cue, sank the seven in the side. "I ain't heartless," he said, "so stop staring." He dropped the chalk, snagged it with the hooks. "Stupid's what that is. All I'm saying."

Shrugging, Amnaj drifted to the cash register near Castro.

Nails blew chalk from the tip. "Stupid gets fucked. How it is."

Nokyung went through the blade of afternoon light let in by SevenEight as he went out. She sat with Katia. Amnaj leaned on his elbows. Castro clicked the pen, inserted it into the notebook, and sipped the iced Corona. Joom went past, spread her hands on the pool table rails.

Nokyung, a flip-flop braced on the floor. "What do you bother my uncle for?"

"Don't you see it?" Katia said. "He has an eye for Maria."

Nokyung had seen it. The way he fawned over her, his huge, sweaty body presiding over her. The blushing fright in Maria's eyes. She saw that, too. But she knew, as well, that it was the way of the man. "What do you care," she said, "the way you carry on with your boyfriend?"

"I protect her," Katia said. "And you better watch Joom. She'll get hurt."

Nokyung licked her lips, her mouth hard and dry. Behind her, Joom chatted with Nails, who was working around her.

"I've watched her," Katia said. "But you don't pay attention." She glanced at Amnaj. "He's a good one, your uncle. But not when it comes to something that pays well. They'll come after him one day. He doesn't have the money and won't be able to stop them."

Nokyung felt her face tighten. "Who comes after him?"

"Forget it," she said. "Nothing you can do about it." Her gaze drifted toward the television. Her teeth scraped her bottom lip. She gestured at Joom. "There's your worry. I don't mean Nails. Nails is all right. But even with him, you can see how she is. Light and teasing, she's fun for these old men. They love her. Sexy sweet in ways she isn't aware of. They love her, all right, and she loves all the attention. And in here that's dangerous."

Nokyung glared at Katia. Wanted to tell her to mind her own business but knew she'd meant well, and, besides, it was true. She sighed and turned away. A dull sensation whirled in her breast. Spun downward and pressed on her stomach. She concentrated on the wet gray pictures of flooded streets and wind-battered buildings on the television. The camera's focus was intimate. Like something happening next door, though the storm-slashed shoreline was six hundred miles away.

Joom Janpong

THE SCENT OF RED curry filled her nostrils. Joom set down the knife and dumped quartered eggplant into a bowl and pinched a bit of rice into her mouth. Picked up a spoon and sipped the curry. Yawned. Sometimes she was confused, everything happening all at once, and so fast. She chopped cilantro and sprinkled it over spicy beef in a bowl. I'm a good girl, but she'd just gotten up from a damp, smelly bed and rushed to work. A naked man had brushed his teeth in the bathroom. He'd kissed her. She chopped green onion. Heard a cry, turned toward the television. Amnaj and Maria stood shoulder-to-shoulder beneath the screen and stared at ships enduring the onslaught of powerful waves. Henry or Steve, that was the guy's name. She could never remember. He came to the bar the night before, said he was the regional manager of a company selling fine jewelry. Made her laugh. Bought her chocolate cakes and flatliners until she could hardly stand. Hair smelling sweet like vanilla. Made her laugh, and he wasn't married. Held up his hand. See? She scooped green onion and sprinkled it over the spicy beef. Wore a ring on his pinky. Silver with gems. She touched it. Real? Gave her a look, Would I lie to you?—and she giggled, and he wasn't married. He ordered beer. She thrust her hip out. He folded tips into her pocket. Ordered purple hooters and copper camels. Two each. Drink up, he'd said. And she woke up in a dank hotel room, bare legs sticky and tangled in a smelly sheet. Amnaj said it would be easy. Men are everywhere,

he said, and they like Asian girl. He said the men were handsome and rich. All Americans are rich, he said. Introduced her
to his friends. Skin rough like coconuts and mouths redolent
and rotten as fruit. She recoiled instantly, and Nokyung looked
sour. Nokyung had closed up, wrapped herself in a hard shell.
Amnaj said, Never mind her. She won't get a man, but you will.
The Thai ladies had come, too. They gossiped with lips wet with
saliva. Skin shiny and red with makeup. Naked, he brushed his
teeth, Henry or Steve or Raymond. She couldn't remember. A
sagging body. Wrinkled like soiled laundry. A smell like medicine. Amnaj became angry when she pouted and complained
that they were too old. Give me the money, he said. She handed it over, some of it. The rest hidden away. He said she could
make more. Would give her a return. SevenEight stared from
the bar, his face shrouded in smoke. She never saw the money again and gave him less each time. And when he ran out of
friends, he found strangers at the bar. Introduced them like old
pals. She stripped romaine, moistened it, displayed it on a platter. A light flashed over her hands. SevenEight went outside.
Steve or Raymond packed his things in a torn suitcase. Naked,
he folded shirts into a suitcase. Checkout's noon, he said. His
balls hung like rotten plums. Two top teeth were missing. He
pressed a thick retainer into his mouth. Don't be picky, Amnaj said. She wiped the knife with a soft cloth. Nokyung came
around the bar and sat next to Katia, and Katia smacked the
counter and shouted at Maria. Don't be picky, Amnaj said. Get
the green card. Then divorce him if you want. A nice man for
a husband, that's all she wanted. And Nokyung didn't try. She
pouted. Wrapped herself up tight like a banana blossom. Went

around cleaning. Too busy for them. The men saw Nokyung, bought her drinks, and she refused them. Joom knew the trick. Nokyung repelled them, made herself plain. At first, she felt anger toward Nokyung. Then resentment. She cried inwardly at the serrated edge of rancor sliding up and down her spine. Steve or Raymond or Ethan, she couldn't remember, stood naked packing socks in a suitcase, telling her checkout's at noon, staring at the cell phone ringing on the nightstand. She looked, too. Looked at the ringing phone. Looked at him. Saw the pinky ring glinting. He wasn't married. She wiped a scrim of sweat from her breasts. Looked at him. He looked at the phone and smiled with embarrassment and took it in hand and motioned, Just a minute, and moved away, like he would go into the closet. She turned, nearly dropping a dish. Jimmy Nails shouted, and everyone stared at him. At the end of the bar, she stood near Castro, who glanced, then returned to the television, where the hull of a boat was bobbing in rough, gray water. Katia and Nokyung glared at each other. Amnaj skittered away. She slipped past Katia and Nokyung to the end of the pool table. Raymond or Ethan spoke softly into the cell phone. He moved away. Spoke in whispers. Glanced as if she were a bed lamp he'd forgotten to switch off, turned away, whispered into the phone. Turned so that he could look at her nakedness and hide his mouth at the same time. He stood naked, hair withered like a winter rice field. She pulled the sheet around her neck. Jimmy Nails shouted again, not at her, at no one, at everyone, striking out. His pool cue lanced outward. Something deep and painful in the tone. Ethan or Jerry stood naked, dangling, drooping, an old slung coat on a hook, and whispered into the phone. I'm in a meeting, he lied into the phone. He said, honey, into the phone. He said he was in a meeting. He said, honey. The damp sheet around her neck covered her body, scratched her nipples. She watched, watched his mouth whispering. Lips like broken twigs. Heard her name. Heard Nokyung calling her. She leaned against the pool table. Jimmy Nails bent down, an aiming eye toward the corner pocket, the cue gliding between the hooks. Beyond him, Nokyung slid off the stool, motioned, Come, Come. Ethan or Jerry or Owen, she couldn't remember, set down the phone, smiled, knelt on the bed, and kissed her fore-head. He called her baby, not honey. He had the eyes of an eel.

Joom followed Nokyung to a small table in the corner. The door opened. Blasko staggered in, pant cuffs tattered, dragging on the floor. He stood blinking. Amnaj told him to shut the door. He couldn't catch it, swayed against it, finally pulled it to with both hands.

"You won't get a husband," Nokyung said. "Not how you carry on."

"And you will?"

Blasko crossed the floor, chair to chair.

"I'm not looking for one."

"Didn't we come here for that?"

Nokyung sighed. "Huh . . . on the plane. That was before. They use you. They laugh at you. Call you names."

Joom crossed her arms. Her mouth felt heavy. She pushed her tongue against her teeth to open it, but it wouldn't budge. Nails stood nearby chalking the cue. He watched the door, waiting for the Mexicans. She liked how he treated them, beat them, gave back their money. Like he had no use for it.

He stood large in the room, and no one bothered him.

Nokyung's fingers snug on her arm.

"I wish to find a husband, too, ตัวเอง. The whole flight I dreamed of it. But you see how it is."

"You don't try."

"No nice man comes here."

"I give them a chance."

"They play with you."

Joom looked at the television. Maria was laughing behind the bar. Blasko sat on a stool, his head barely upright. A few crumpled dollars held between crooked fingers.

"I will find a man who treats me good."

"You won't, ตัวเอง."

Joom sighed. "Maybe in another life I ran away from my husband. Maybe it is my fate to be tricked."

"I'm going home," Nokyung said. "We can save and go."

"I have no money." Joom watched her sister's face. It was already suspicious, staid and suspicious. Her skin clear, burnished deep with concern. "I wanted to ask you . . ."

"Oh, Joom."

"It's not for me." She glanced across the room.

Nokyung turned. "Uncle? What does he—"

"Not much." She clasped her hands on the table. "But too much."

"He borrows?"

She nodded. "He says he has lost it."

"You can not give him money."

"How can I say no to my uncle?"

She heard the clatter of the balls from a hard break. Jimmy Nails stroked his jaw and seemed to be staring at her. She turned to the television. Maria leaned against the rail. She looked strangely sad beneath her thick, black hair.

"Don't give him any more, ตัวเอง. Promise me."

Joom sighed.

Nokyung carried a bottle to Castro.

Joom saw a shadow. Jimmy Nails across the table. He sat down. "Don't worry about it," he said.

She pouted. "She thinks I'm a bad girl."

"You ain't no bad girl," he said. "I seen a bad one, and you ain't one." He spoke without looking at her. His hook scraped lightly across the table. "Tell you what. Blame circumstance. Blame luck. How it treats you. And beats you."

She reached across the table and looped her fingers in the hooks. Lifted them up. "And you?"

Now he looked at her. Then he laughed. "Shit. Sometimes it just plain defeats you."

Then she saw the scars on his arms. Long welts like mountain ranges rising from the skin. She looked at him, about to ask, but he shook his head. "You know most men'll kill themselves with a gun. I ain't got no gun."

"It's OK now?"

"Like I said."

She released him. "Least you have this. I see how you clean up on the Mexicans."

He opened and closed the hook. "Nigger should see my ass on a Skilsaw."

Nokyung Janpong

NOKYUNG HATED THE BAR, but the afternoons were all right. Before the smoke. Before the rambunctious and slurry chatter. When the air was sweetened by jasmine rice, spicy curry, stir-fried basil, and strips of grilled chicken. Joom arranged the buffet on a long side table against the far wall. Rice, centered and prominent. Plastic spoons and forks. A tower of paper plates. Every night a feast. Free for the patrons. Amnaj said it brought them customers. It makes them happy. But Nokyung saw that it cost much more to prepare the food than it was worth.

Once a week or more, the Thai ladies came in. They were the ones who had made it, who ran businesses in town, and who set up booths at the temple during Songkran, Loy Krathong, and the king's birthday. They'd all married into money, to lawyers, doctors, military colonels. So, the stories ran, but who knew what was exaggerated? Nokyung and Joom watched them closely and gossiped about them as much as they were themselves gossiped about.

The Thai ladies went through the bar rearranging tables, a herd of structured dresses, cluster jackets, and gold and diamond clips. Sometimes they sat outside to gossip under the stars while the sea breeze slowly undid their hair and streaked their faces. They were ready to introduce a "good" man to Nokyung and Joom, and to warn them who they should stay away from.

Amnaj attended to them, drank with them. Nokyung saw

what he was after. He needed their daughters and nieces to fill up En La Playa. He needed them because the men would come. The daughters and nieces made them happy. And the ribs and papaya salad and spring rolls were free.

Nokyung relished the afternoons with Castro at the end of the bar writing quietly in his notebook. The music a low drone, the lighting as pleasant and serene as the long, thin, and silent halls of sacred temples, where rows of golden Buddhas sat cross-legged on golden daises. If it would only stay that way. But a man or two, strangers, might drop in wearing suits and ties. Clean-shaven men in polos and checkered shorts. While she was taking orders she heard the chatter of Maria and Joom. They inventoried clothing brands, calculated wallet sizes, figured out the odds of attraction and ways of getting noticed.

Amnaj scrutinized the men from his perch at the bar. Or he appeared from the back, seeming to have some sense that possibility had entered his establishment. He gave them a father's dangerous, mistrustful eye, pronouncing some men no good instantly or, by not saying anything, letting it play out. Or if the Thai ladies were present, he sat with them, and they worked it out for him, cackling and chirping from their gossipy nests.

Nokyung hated this moment most of all. If the men went away after a few drinks, Amnaj came immediately and scolded her for putting on a sour face. She felt her body crimp, all but disappear, and busied herself as soon as possible with cleaning counters and arranging napkins and tip jars.

If she could only hold onto the afternoon, she could stand the nuisance of being presented a little longer. When the crowds were thin, she dreamed of the hot, dusty smell of Chiang Mai. The outdoor café where she ate sausage flavored with lemon grass. Tuk-tuk chugging along narrow roads. The hazy hill fires of Doi Sutep. She suffered deeply the pain of distance and the pain of memory and, liking neither, swept the floor, wiped the counters, arranged the bottles, and prepared the food to empty herself of feeling.

The afternoons were warm. A salty fragrance blew from the south. They got it ready, and customers arrived singly, in pairs, in groups. They arrived shouting and laughing. Hiding their wallets like treasure or opening them like barbed hooks for unsuspecting fish. Nokyung shuddered each time the door opened. Flinched when they said hello, froze when they touched her freely, and did her best to please her uncle. To do what he said she should do.

She wished hard, but it did not stop evening from gulping down the afternoon or night swallowing the evening. Blasko, an instant pungent smell of a man, searched his pockets for coins. He piled what he could scrounge on the counter. Haggard-looking, expectant, and nothing left for a tip. Dead drunk at closing time. His head on the counter. Or slumped in a dark corner. Katia at the other end of the bar with SevenEight. She shook her head. Her face hard as iron. SevenEight berated her, a stern pointing finger, and she took it. And beyond them, Nails aiming for the corner pocket. A blank-faced Mexican in a torn red shirt standing nearby. His pals against the wall looked on. Turned and spoke to one another with dry smiles. One of them, Joel, came with another man, Flaco. They always came together. They left together.

But they did not seem like they belonged together.

Joel stood casually with a light laugh, a plump baby face, deep, round eyes. Amazed and amused by everything. A bubbling infant enchanted by colorful lights.

The other man, Flaco, seemed to have been torn from coal. Dark and brooding and ruthless—as if his eyes were the sting of the black scorpion. He rarely smiled. His laugh seemed to mock.

What Nokyung found strange was the shadow of recognition on Flaco's face when Maria served them. Maria must have felt it. She went around him, out of her way, when she brought them drinks. Something distressing in her manner. Flaco had a natural sneer to his looks, and that was probably it.

Joel was different. He couldn't take his eyes off Maria. Nokyung could see them together, like a couple. Whether they noticed or not, she saw the spark. Joel, in clothes too large for him, leaning close to whisper to Maria as she passed by. She couldn't see Maria's face but imagined she was blushing, sending out a playful, girlish smile. But she also seemed desperate to escape. A kind of trembling in the legs when she scurried away. And the other man, who Maria did not see, stared at her hard and mean, as if he were determined to remember something.

Nokyung saw things in panorama. Amnaj next to Maria, both staring at the television. He leaned against her, casually, oppressively. Reaching for a plastic straw. A napkin. She stood in acquiescence, in innocence of his intention or inviting it.

The Thai ladies giggled over beef salad and steaming rice, piling it on their plates, and sat huddled around tables. They waved, and she carried bottles of beer on a tray. They tugged her arm, felt along her skin, pulled her down into an empty chair.

Two men came through the door, looking damp. Apparently rain had begun to fall. They found a table.

The Thai ladies became silent with inspection. Soon as they recognized that one of the two men was Reynolds, they laughed. Nokyung felt trapped between their bodies, swamped by their scents. Green ivy, tangerine, ginger root. She searched for Amnaj, hoping he would yell at her to return to work.

"A sad man," Muu said, speaking of Reynolds.

"Wasted," Jiiab said. "Led like a cow by SevenEight."

Muu forked rice onto her spoon. "Katia could step up."

Pook reached across the table for eggplant. "She's as beaten as he is."

Nokyung listened and looked bored.

"You can't blame her," Jiiab said.

"None of them are good," Maew said. "But the one with Reynolds, I've never seen him."

Pook split the eggplant. "Reynolds's superior, I'll bet." She placed half on Muu's plate. "Looks smart."

"Thank you," Muu said. "Smart and pretends he has money. That's too smart."

They all laughed. Nokyung squirmed against their warm, gluey bodies. She wished she could go back to work.

Maew cut beef with her spoon. "It'd be best," she said, "if they went somewhere else."

"Reynolds could take SevenEight." Jiiab crunched the eggplant between her teeth. "So, why doesn't he?"

"Something on him," Pook said.

"Money at the bottom." Muu's spoon shook when she spoke. "You can bet on that."

Nokyung felt Pook's hand close on hers. She resisted irritation, resigned herself to being trapped at the table.

"The new one, Reynolds's superior?" Maew leaned a bit. "He seems too curious about things. Studies the room. Up to something."

Pook squeezed her hand. "A clever one, that's what he is."

"Penniless," Muu said.

They all laughed.

Nokyung jumped when Pook touched her arm. "A clever one, dear. Don't go falling for him."

"I'm not falling for anyone," Nokyung said, making a face.

"She doesn't know what she wants," Maew said. "But we know what they want, don't we? Poor Joom, she can't keep her legs closed."

They all laughed. Nokyung remained silent.

Others came through the door, shaking off rain. Some directly to the food tables. Others straight for the bar.

"I must go." Nokyung rose as if escaping giant crabs.

Castro closed his notebook. SevenEight crossed the room with a cigarette hanging from his mouth. Maria, Katia, and Joom stared at the television. A shattered hull bobbed up and down. Amnaj, from the stock room, scolded and pointed. And suddenly stopped. He stood with the others. He stood staring at the television. The helicopters swarmed over the bodies, bloated like dead fish on the gray, churning surface of the Gulf.

Derek Stickleback

Rain fell on the windshield. High clouds scuttled across the sky. This rain wasn't the coming storm. It was a system crossing the Panhandle from the plains. Stickleback glanced at Reynolds, quiet in the passenger's seat. Not the same man. Preoccupied, staring out the window, his jaw tight. He'd changed since middle school. Nothing like the bully who'd filled Zander Olsen's mouth with Tabasco. Nothing like the brash kid in high school who'd made all-county linebacker. His stint in Afghanistan. He was good going in. Brave. Sure of what he was doing. He'd changed. Not the same man. Stickleback wished Reynolds had come back a braggart. Not this isolated brooder who specialized in the perfunctory. He'd vanished for a while. Stickleback seemed to know very little now about his childhood friend. Only once had Reynolds started to say what had happened. A half-gesture that began with eight combat deaths. Then he'd stopped midsentence and shaken his head.

Stickleback drove easy down the beach highway. Radio set to an all-jazz station. He didn't know anything about jazz, except that it sometimes fit his wind-down mood. Bars and clubs and tall hotels mingled with long sloping dunes of white sand. They went past the park and the fishing pier. He palmed the steering wheel, tugged off his wedding ring.

"Guess I'd better hide the evidence," he said, slipping the ring into his pocket.

Reynolds gazed at him, then out the window, his face alternating light and dark.

"Saw you with Heebner today," Stickleback said. "That guy's a wreck."

Reynolds stroked his jaw. "No wonder, what he's been through."

"Other day I'm down there, and he's staring at those posters he got set up."

"It helps him."

"That's no help." Stickleback rubbed the itch on his bare ring finger. "He needs to get back out or turn in his badge."

Reynolds, face turned away, mumbled into the wet glass of the window. "You don't know the hardship of a man." And chest, head, he touched them in succession.

Stickleback let it drop for a moment. The old Reynolds would have jumped on it, and all for a quick laugh. Heebner wasn't worth talking about, but Reynolds, for whatever reason, had been drawn out, if only a little.

"Staring at pictures won't do him any good, I know that."

"He's an artist," Reynolds said. "Those prints—great works of art, he tells me—help him not to think."

"What I'm saying," Stickleback said, and he passed a slow car. "There's straight thinking and there's Indy 500 thinking—and that man's leading the pack."

"You don't know." The words trailed off, and Stickleback sensed the words were not for him but for someone else.

"And you're all buddy-buddy—so what were you doing with Heebner, anyway?"

"He left his swipe card in the bathroom."

"That's why they stuck him down in armory, where he couldn't do any more harm."

"Don't you ever give a guy a break? The guy's suffered enough."

"You defending him? He didn't do his job, and that's dangerous."

"He was cleared. The armory's self-imposed exile. He's got to work himself back."

"It'll never happen, the guy's a fuck up."

Reynolds turned dark, the lighting or the angle of his head.

"Could happen to anyone," Reynolds said. The volume of his voice nearly lost in the noise of the bar. "Let it go."

Stickleback chuckled. "All right, man, ease up, will you? All I'm saying is that a guy who writes passwords on sticky pads and leaves them out where anyone can find them, well, I don't want that guy looking after my back."

"No one could ever keep up with you."

"What are you saying?"

"Ain't nothing to say." Reynolds wiped fog from the window. "Let it go."

They fell silent. The radio jazz was infused with a tenor sax that held a lunar tone. The rain and wipers forced a rhythm on the indulgence of the drums.

"What about this year?" Stickleback said, bringing them back to a conversation they'd started earlier.

Reynolds shook his head. "I like where I'm at."

"Come on, man, you staying corporal all your life? You've been in long enough. Tell you what. I'm recommending you for a shield. Like it or not. And that gets you in. Easy."

Reynolds stared out the window.

Stickleback saw a bent sign past Reynolds's careworn face. "That it?"

"Yeah," Reynolds said. "Turn here."

He wheeled the SUV into the lot, backed into a space near a wooden fence. They walked through the slackening rain. The seashell matte of the parking lot crunched beneath their feet. "A dump," Stickleback said, looking at the cinderblock building.

At one time, plaster had encased the building, but now the plaster was cracked. Large gashes left the block exposed. A light through the window blinked on and off.

"Won't find better food," Reynolds said.

They entered. Eyes adjusted. Found a table. Stickleback rubbed his ring finger, relieving the itch that encircled it. Television flickered with news of the storm.

"The man at the end of the bar," Reynolds said, nodding. "He's the owner. A good man to know."

"How's that?"

"He's not on sides." Reynolds seemed to be searching for someone. "Or he's on both sides."

"A straddler. Got no use for it." Stickleback stared at the dark corner past the bar. A long light hung dim over chalk-dusty baize.

"There's a mystery," Reynolds said.

"Reading my mind, are you?"

"Ever since you stole my girl in middle school."

Stickleback laughed. Did the sparkle of the old Reynolds

slip out or was it the Mexican coming their way, her hair filtering the light?

"God, I can't remember her name," Reynolds said, and he looked sick again, desperate.

"Jeannie, Janie, Joanie—don't beat yourself up over it. That was a long time ago."

"His name is Nails. Jimmy Nails," Reynolds said. "That death-look on his face. That's normal wear."

Stickleback saw the cue sliding through the prostheses. Face calm and settled. Nails stepped away from the pool table and motioned to a Mexican in a ball cap.

"So, listen, Ray." Stickleback turned, wanted to get inside his friend. "I don't need a tour of the bar. I wanted to tell you—"

"Hello, Maria." Reynolds's face brightened. A dark girl stood there, hand on hip. Light from the television gave her hair a brindled radiance.

Reynolds held up two fingers. "Dos."

Maria nodded and went away. Reynolds watched her go. Stickleback saw a flicker in Reynolds's eyes, an unusual brightness, but it was hard to tell if it were only the flashes of television and bar lights.

"I think she's sweet on you," Stickleback said.

Reynolds moved napkins on the table, shook his head. "A sweet girl, yes, but not on me. She works hard but hardly says a word."

Stickleback looked around. Reynolds, he realized, was too intent on pushing away, and let the matter drop. "I guess I'd be careful if I were illegal."

Reynolds shrugged. "I don't ask questions in here."

"But you can count them, can't you?" Stickleback noticed the volume of his voice lowering. "Like one more bus stop on the immigration circuit."

Stickleback draped an arm over his chair. Reynolds hunched forward. Stickleback sensed, though he could not see it, that Reynolds had his hands clasped between his knees and was wringing them. Just past him a woman came toward them. Unlike the others, she wasn't cringing with fear or avoiding eye contact. She stopped a moment at a table of women, laughed at something they said, shrugged or shook her head, and then strode forward and slid into the chair next to Reynolds. "What's up, baby?"

Stickleback noted something intimate on Reynolds's face, but there was more. His face wilted almost immediately. Maria arrived with the beer. Katia said something in Spanish. Her tone harsh. Maria's lip tightened, and she scurried away. Reynolds reached for the mug.

Katia motioned toward the bar. "SevenEight wants to know who this man is," she said. "Who should I say? Detective, undercover agent, spy?" She winked.

Stickleback smiled. Had he not been informed already that Amnaj was the owner he would have guessed Katia ran things. The confidence in her voice, the certainty of her manner. At home. In control. Yet, her voice slipped with hesitancy when she spoke of the man at the bar. A subtle darkness stretched across her face.

Past Katia, the man she'd mentioned, SevenEight, sat slack on a bar stool, a cigarette hanging from his lips. He pretended to watch the television. Slowly stroked an uneven jaw. Longer and longer, the glances lingered. Then he was staring. Stickleback knew the type. Brash, self-important. A bully. Push-to-shove, a coward. But until that push, he racked up cruelty points from the timid. That's what he saw crossing Katia's face when she'd said his name.

"Investigator," Stickleback said, working up a disarming smile. "But relax. I'm off duty. My friend here says this is a good bar with good people."

Katia gazed back with mock surprise. "He must be talking about some other bar," she said with a light laugh. "And anyway," she continued, touching Reynolds's arm, "what's slowing you down, baby, that you aren't Investigator like your friend?"

"Told you to leave it alone."

Stickleback expected Reynolds to blow it off but not with such heat.

Katia looked unfazed. She turned to Stickleback. "He's nicer when he's had a few too many. Opposite of most people."

"You seem to know each other," Stickleback said.

Reynolds exhaled loudly, spoke to Katia. "Don't you have something to do?"

"A little too well," Katia said to Stickleback.

No loss of composure, she wiped hair from her eyes. Then a shadow crossed the table. SevenEight behind Katia. A hand on her shoulder. A little too firm, Stickleback thought, rankled by SevenEight's presence. The man's face was covered with scuzzle and scars.

"Take off," SevenEight said to Katia.

She was up and off with a slap on the ass.

SevenEight straddled a chair. He lifted Reynolds's chin. "What you doing here, boyfly? Ain't I tell you stay away?"

"Yes, sir," Reynolds said.

SevenEight glanced at Stickleback. "Don't get dicked up about this," he said. "We cool."

Stickleback suppressed irritation. Nothing but a cheap thug. All done up in a dirty wife-beater, ratty button up, and dull grillz. But it didn't make sense. Reynolds, sheepish, body limp, cowed. No sense at all. Maybe Reynolds was gone, the one he'd known. He thought of the looks Reynolds had exchanged with Katia. What that was about. Now this. He worked it over. They'd been together in the military. Maybe that was it. But Reynolds associating with trash stretched the imagination. That submissive posture. That wasn't Reynolds. Maybe he was gone. The one he'd known. He sat there. "Yes, sir," every time SevenEight spoke. Stickleback felt heat rushing through his neck.

SevenEight turned, looked at Katia, turned back, thumbed over his shoulder. A whistle. "That some fine, pumpy ass, Captain."

Stickleback felt heat in his face.

SevenEight threw his chest out. "Shit. Nigger get a dick in that? Hole suck you right in. Won't let go without no jaws-of-life. I'm telling you—pop!"

Reynolds sat slumped, a ripple of pain across his face.

"Shut the fuck up," Stickleback said. He planted his feet, leaned forward.

SevenEight laughed. Moved his shoulders up and down.

Made fists, spun them, comic imitation of a fighter. "Nigger here got him some balls." Shot a glance at Reynolds, as if he hadn't made his point. "Yes, sir, big, fat, bouncy balls."

Stickleback pressed the table, ready to rise. SevenEight shoved back. The chair clattered to the floor. Then began laughing and pointing. "Flinch! I saw it, but it's OK. We cool." He clapped, laughing, turned toward the bar. The chair down where it had fallen. Stickleback stood, hands on the table. He saw someone rising out of the gloom. From the table of old women. She came in a rush. Swooped down, set the chair upright. He turned to Reynolds.

"What the fuck was that? What the fuck's the matter with you?"

He shook Reynolds, chin dug deep in his chest.

"Calling that bastard sir like you're his galley slave. What's with this 'yes sir' crap?"

Reynolds took a deep breath. "Sorry. Shouldn't have brought you."

"The hell—" Stickleback was interrupted by the scraping sound of the chair, the girl pushing it under the table. He looked at her and frowned. She had the dreariest face he'd ever seen.

"Nokyung," Reynolds said, motioning. Then a gesture to Stickleback. "We go back. Reason I'm on the force."

Stickleback shifted into pleasantries. "That's your doing, pal. Nice to meet you."

He extended his hand. She stared at it. Not much effort to return the smile, either. More like biting it out. She dipped her head, hair scattering around her face, and launched away.

She disappeared around the counter. Head barely above it. Behind her, the owner and the girl who'd served them looking at the television. The picture gray and stormy. Stickleback sat back down.

"Shy?"

"Complete opposite of her sister." Reynolds searched the room. "Over there by the food tables."

"A cutey."

"Wear a condom."

Reynolds should be laughing at his own joke, Stickleback thought, but he sits in a shape of leaden flatness. No longer angry, he decided to let the incident go.

"They call her Boom Boom," Reynolds said, his mouth barely opening.

"Maybe why that other one's got the sneer. A little sibling jealousy."

"I feel sad for her."

"Sad?"

"She doesn't know what she's doing. None of them do. They're thrown into this on blade-thin promises."

"Yeah, what was that? I offered my hand. Friendly enough, and she's backing away like I'm a scorpion or something."

Reynolds lifted the beer. The mug had sat so long the suds were gone.

"Not their custom. They're Thai. They avoid public touching."

Stickleback nodded, watching. Nokyung set mugs onto the counter, one after the other. She worked like a machine. Her hand appeared with a filled glass, set it on a tray, dropped out of sight, then rose with another.

"Long fingers."

Reynolds turned toward the bar.

"You'll have to check them out doing their dance. When no one's here, nothing to do, they'll go over there, the two of them. Do that thing with their fingers bending back. Graceful and all that. They actually look happy."

Stickleback sipped his beer slowly. Nokyung, he observed, kept herself compact, physically secretive, socially aloof. She stood small at a table with several beef bodies and crew tops. They were giving her a time. She looked lonely, a far-off gaze, like waiting to catch a bus.

"Another custom, if you're thinking anything," Reynolds said. "Don't touch their heads. They'll get ballistic on you. Just don't do it."

Stickleback noticed that Reynolds spoke in a hurry, as if avoiding saying something else.

"Bizarre. What's that about?"

Reynolds wiped his mouth, leaned in. "A Buddhist thing. The head's the high part of the body. Sacred. Grave insult to go around touching a Thai head."

Stickleback heard the clap of pool balls, a groan from the Mexican shooter, who handed over cash to Nails. Reynolds seemed to have gotten lost in his own thoughts. Barely moved. Seemed to be working up courage.

"Guess they're all here for cards," Stickleback said.

Reynolds turned slowly. Returning from a gray realm.

"Sure," he said. "All of them except Katia. She's got hers."

"Got her a husband? The owner? They look good together."

Reynolds smiled. Stickleback wondered what he'd said.

"Not a chance. Like left and right, those two."

"That's balance."

"Call it what you want."

He watched Reynolds take up the mug. Breathe over it, gaze into it, a yellowy crystal ball. Working up courage. He was certain that's what he was doing. But for what? Over Reynolds's shoulder, the Thai sisters stood next to each other by the food table. The one called Joom swayed, a little out of time with the music, but the glow on her face made up for her lack of rhythm. The other one stood somnolent, her funereal features made darker still by the lack of lighting near the table.

A flash of light in the corner of his eye. He turned toward the pool table. Reynolds had said Nails was a mystery. The hooks themselves, raw and medieval, evoking images of Dark Age torture. That was mystery enough. But what else? He studied Nails's face. The scars on his brows. Something familiar about them, but he couldn't place it. Not a local mystery. Nothing ever happened in Midsummer.

He turned back to Reynolds. His lips moving, going over something. They'd been silent long enough. He coughed. Reynolds looked up.

"Listen, Lieutenant," Reynolds said. "About SevenEight. About what happened. The man's only playing. He's a playa, get it? A gansta in his tiny hip-hop dreams. But odd, you know? This thing for me. Harmless, Lieutenant. Forget about it."

A shout from the bar. Everyone turned. The television glowed like an eye. People clinging to debris in the rough water. Someone yelled, Where are they? Someone yelled back,

Southwest of Cape Coral. Soon the pictures became repetitive. The same long shot of a Coast Guard cutter on the water. A helicopter flattening the waves. Soaked, puny bodies clinging to planks and foam cushions. Attention drifted.

Stickleback wanted to say something to Reynolds. But the man was deflated. He decided not now. Another time. "Let's get out of here. We've got an early day."

"You go on," Reynolds said. "I'll catch a ride."

"Come on, man, it's late. You don't belong here."

Reynolds looked heavy, sad. "You never been outside the wire, man. You don't get it."

Stickleback looked at SevenEight. "He's scum. I understand that."

"Let it go."

Stickleback tossed a dollar down. "Suit yourself."

He drove along wet streets. Drove in silence. The stars had reappeared, glistening after the rain. He felt irritated. Reynolds was right, of course, he couldn't understand, not in the way he had meant it. But there was more. And he couldn't place it. But this wasn't the irritation. Reynolds had served well, he was certain, but no one thanked him for his service. He'd chosen En La Playa as his haunt, where it was even more certain no one knew he was a man who deserved thanks.

Nokyung Janpong

"Hear any more?" She spooned rice porridge into bowls. Sprinkled shredded pork over it. A bit of ginger and crushed peppers.

Amnaj rubbed under his arms, pulled on a muscle shirt, and sat at the table. "I heard they were all dead."

"All dead?" She looked up. "No. Not all dead. We saw them floating in the water. They were waving their arms."

He shrugged. "That's what I heard."

"No," she said. "Who told you that?"

He sighed. "Who cares? They're a hundred miles away. You girls go on and on about it like they're living right next door. Like it's any of our business."

She turned the spoon around the bowl. "Grumpy, aren't you? Go back to sleep."

He rotated his head. Groaned. Loosened his neck.

She spooned porridge into her mouth.

"I've been out this morning," she said. "You won't believe how clear and bright it is. It's hard to imagine. It reminds me of the sky over the Kok River."

He broke green onion into the porridge. "You don't know the storm. It will come soon. It will come hard."

She watched him. He ate too fast. She spooned more into his bowl. "I'm homesick, Uncle."

He looked over the spoon, a slight head shake. Then resumed eating. Like she hadn't said a thing.

"I am saving money," she said. "And I spoke with Jit this morning while you slept. She will let me make money at the dry cleaner."

He sighed so hard the table napkins fluttered. Tossed down the spoon. "And what about me, what the about the bar? Talk about going home. About finding more work. Don't you think I want to save? Joom wants to save, too. But she shares. That's what she does. Do you share with your uncle? Don't be selfish."

She felt pressure at the tip of her tongue. Where it mashed against her teeth, the binding of her lips. Joom shared. That's right. For gambling debts. She wanted to throw that at him but couldn't. Afraid to shame him. And he would tell her mother and shame her.

He began eating again. "Now, Joom," he said. "That's a good girl. Helps me out plenty. Never complains. I bet she's homesick, too. Don't hear about that, do you? And do you see how she tries for a husband? And what do you do but try to get more money and never share a cent. How's that for stingy, thinking only of yourself?"

She toyed with the porridge. Her mother had said that her brother had fallen in with a bad crowd. He was younger then, she'd said, and had gone off to Chiang Mai. There were gangs. The word frightened her. Young men on motorbikes. Young working men without work. Uncle was one of them. A desperate look on his face when he returned to Mae Ai late one night. Debts from gambling. They were coming for him. Her mother hid him. An anxious time. They were told to pretend he wasn't there. A terrifying time. Her mother gave him money, found passage to Bangkok. Here he was, same man, older, but the same. The secret way he slipped rolled bills to SevenEight. The way they cast stern looks at everyone, challenges to anyone with questions about what they were up to. A sad, squalid picture.

She lowered her eyes. "What do you need, Uncle?"

He slammed his hand on the table. "Don't dare insult me! Am I a beggar that I must crawl to you with what I need? I own the bar that pays you. I don't need anything from you. What do you do? I know it. I know what you do. You squeeze that money so tight. Every hard penny of it. Trying to squeeze the blood from the crab."

Her face simmered with agitation. "I send money to my mother—"

"You go about it all wrong, แม่หลานสาว."

He stirred the last of the porridge, came up with a bite. Then shook the empty spoon at her.

"Joom knows what to do," he said. "Do like her. Find a rich man. Marry him. Then my sister will be happy, and I will be happy. Do that, and we'll all be happy. It's not so hard."

Tears welled in her eyes. Her uncle appeared blurry.

"But I don't like them," she said. "I don't feel anything."

He stared at her, shaking his head. He motioned that she should come with him. They walked outside the bar, stood near the barbecue pit.

"Look at me," he said.

She looked.

"You're a decent girl, Nokyung. My favorite niece. You look surprised. Jing jing—it's true!"

She didn't believe it, but her body felt soothed. She searched for its source. The breeze. The shade of pines. The dunes. Beyond, the flat, green water. She looked at her uncle. His unshaven face red like a setting sun.

"You don't need a feeling," he said. "This is for the family. To keep us going strong. Not just me. All of us. Your mother, too. So, you find a man with money who is maybe OK, and you marry him. Get the green card. And then if you don't like him, you get divorced." He took a deep breath, seemed to scan the horizon as if he needed something from it, an inspiration. Another deep breath, rooted in the base of his lungs. "All you have to do is make a good show of it. Do that?"

Her lips were crushed together. It hurt to part them. "Yes, Uncle," she said. She put her hands together and bowed. She felt as if she'd been tossed from a mountain. She wanted to scream. But she was afraid.

They stood a moment longer. Then she dug the keys to the Suzuki Swift from her pocket. Jit expected her at the dry cleaners that morning. She looked at her uncle. Then at the cloudless sky. "Doesn't seem at all like a storm's coming, does it?"

Joom Janpong

In the evening, a light rain fell. Joom was deciding whether to put the papaya salad next to the rice or next to the garlic chicken when a very fat man came into the bar. He sat at a table and set down a stack of bills. On top he placed a gold money clip, and he looked up. He looked around. It was all for show. The face of an owl. Eyes one way. Then the other.

She watched Nokyung, chatting with Castro. Watched her eyes drift toward the fat man. Castro also turned toward the fat man. She couldn't see Castro's expression, just the soft shake of his head. He didn't know the fat man.

Past stoop-shouldered patrons at the other end of the counter, Katia held Maria by the arm. They had been watching television but had turned. Katia clutched Maria's arm. A tight and protective grip, and why? Katia's mouth moved rapidly, sharply. Maria stared at the fat man. Katia must have been saying, "Do you understand? Do you hear me?" because Maria nodded vigorously several times.

Jimmy Nails didn't seem to notice anything but the glide of the pool cue.

Amnaj emerged from the back room. He stopped abruptly. Broke into a smile. Came waving an arm toward the fat man. Stood by the table, awaiting acknowledgement. The fat man, as if just now noticing Amnaj, looked up. His face focused on Amnaj, but his gaze traveled across the room. She thought it was the light making her uncle's frame shake as he stood motioning with his hand at Nokyung. Then again, gazing around the room. The gaze settled on her. She turned to the food, began arranging it all over again.

Then Amnaj was next to her. "Let Maria serve him." His eyes were hard, dark. "Katia and Maria will serve him."

Joom glanced past Amnaj's shoulder. "It's my area, Uncle. And you see what's on the table."

"Not tonight." The voice was stern.

"Who is he?"

"Never mind," he said. "Maria and Katia will take that table. You understand? Don't go near."

"But, who is he?"

He opened his mouth, closed it. "Do as you're told."

She made a noise, a grunt, to let him know she'd heard, and she was unhappy.

Amnaj strode away. A sense of urgency in his manner. She didn't have time to reflect further. Several men entered. They shouted and waved. Some pushed to the counter. Some crowded around the table of food. She stepped aside and let them at it. They grabbed bowls. Grabbed plates. Spoke of spices. Spoke of smells. They joked and laughed. Asked questions. She must have heard them. She must have answered. Not until Maria crossed her line of sight did she realize she was staring at the fat man and the stack of bills. Maria set down a drink. He flicked a fat finger at the stack. Maria took a few bills. Flicked again. Maria hesitated but took a few more. Her face bloomed into a smile as she went back to the counter.

"What got you all in a beat-up mood?"

She turned. Blasko. A paper plate shaking in upturned hands. Tall and unshaven. Shirt ripped at the collar. He reeked of alcohol. She looked away.

"Everyone a little jittery tonight," he said. "Even old Amnaj. What's he upset about?"

She glared at Blasko. "Nothing."

Blasko was wretched. Angular, bony, a smell of oily streets and whiskey.

"Don't look like nothing."

"He wants us to get husbands, that's all. We've been here long enough, he says."

Blasko's teeth were brown and deformed. Those he had left. "Pretty girl like you can't find a husband? I don't believe it."

"Not a good husband." She shouldered away from Blasko. Barely able to speak, the letdown of losing the table, of having to watch Maria take handfuls of bills from the table that should have been hers. Her voice felt tiny. "And time's up for us."

Blasko came around, blocked her view. He seemed to have something in his eye. He kept blinking. Or he was passing out. His eyelids, green with dirt. She wished he'd move on, get some food or a drink or something.

"Up for what?" he said, still blinking.

She was tired of him. She was trying to think of a way to get money from the table. She shot Blasko a hard look. "Are you stupid? How long have we been here?"

Blasko stroked his lower lip with his tongue. His tongue, gray, mottled.

"Well," he said, as if truly pondering the question. "I don't remember. But I think I see. The visa's up. I bet that's it."

"Of course not," she said, wishing she hadn't said any-thing. She stood silently and fumed. He smelled bad, and he was interrupting her thought.

"Why don't you get some food before it gets cold," she said.

He laughed. "That's what I came up here for, but you started talking about a husband," he said.

"I did?"

He laughed again. "I don't know. You said your time was up. Don't know what you're in such a hurry for. Unless it's the visa. Bet that's it. But a fine girl such as you could have just about anybody. So I wouldn't worry none."

She glowered at him. "You are stupid, aren't you? Not just drunk but stupid. Get some food before it gets cold."

He smiled softly. "Yeah," he said. "I gotcha. Don't you worry none. Won't tell no one. Not a word, not a soul. And if it comes to it, you can always marry me. I ain't the best catch. But I am reliable."

He laughed, brushed up against her arm, and went to load a plate with papaya salad.

She frowned. His stink on her body. She rushed off to the bathroom to wipe the smell away with wet paper towels. Stood looking in the cracked mirror. Felt the gritty tile beneath her flip-flops. Disinfectant and urine mingled with memories, or sparked them, of the night market in Chiang Mai. The dim lighting like a wet dawn. She felt sleepy and closed her eyes. Maew came through the door. She wore a lavender ruched skirt and a scooped neck blouse. She dashed into a stall.

"You won't make money in here," Maew called out.

Joom turned. Maew's feet, pigeon-toed inside polished low pumps, were visible beneath the stall door. "Who is the fat man, Maew? The one who came in tonight?"

"A lizard," she said. "A lizard with gold in his pockets."

"My uncle was afraid of him."

"As well he should be," she said. The toilet roll cranked. "Samuel Dupuis is not for you, honey."

The toilet flushed. Maew came out with a lipstick tube ready at the mouth. She leaned into the mirror. "Come to the restaurant. I'll introduce you to a man you will like."

"I have never seen him before, but everyone seems to know him, and my uncle is afraid of him."

She pressed her lips together, touched her hair. She turned.

"Maybe you don't need to know everything about your uncle, เด็กเอ้ย. He told you to stay away from Dupuis. Stay away. Come to the restaurant. I have a man good for you."

They left the bathroom together. Joom took orders for beer and shots from a group of men in bowling shirts. They made room for her between them. An arm prowled around her thigh. They laughed, and she laughed and took their orders. Shots all around. And you, too, they shouted. She giggled, pushed off the sneaking arm. Turned and feeling, as she turned, their eyes on her, their eyes mapping her shape to theirs. They shouted something, all of them, more or less. She knew what they meant, what they wanted, and she kept going.

She passed Blasko sprawled at the bar. SevenEight must have come in while she was in the bathroom. He nodded, lifted a finger, the shape of a gun, aimed it at her. She blew him off, then went a little out of the way to pass Dupuis's table.

He flowed over the chair like globs of ice cream scooped onto a tiny cone. She saw the money, green and stacked on the table, the gold clip on top. Nudged a napkin from the tray and stooped to pick it up. Under the table, Dupuis's calves inflated his pants. A foot tapped to a trip-hop tune. She touched the table as she rose. His face, swollen, bloated. She met his eyes, wide and tarnished like spoons and recessed in fatty sockets. He stuck a hand out. The fast glint of a silver ring startled her, and she froze.

His hand still over the table. He waved it. "Leave me hanging?"

When he spoke, the fat around his mouth convulsed. She thought he was smiling but couldn't tell. She reached for the hand and instantly heard Amnaj's voice from across the room.

Dupuis turned. "Don't let him bother you." He snatched her hand and pulled her closer. Then turned his head toward Amnaj who was making his way across the bar. Dupuis kissed her fingers. His lips were rubbery, like squid.

She giggled, then turned at a shadow.

"This is not your area," Amnaj said, speaking harshly in Thai. "Go, go! Get drinks for your customers."

Joom slipped her hand from Dupuis's grip, which had tightened, the silver ring a cold cube of ice against her skin. She tugged hard to free herself. Bowed to Amnaj. Glanced at Dupuis. A fat cheek rose and uncovered a strange smile. She went away wiping her hand and the clammy sensation against her shorts. She could not help thinking that Dupuis had a tricky smile. Still, the money on the table, loose and scattered like leaves of sweet cabbage, seduced the eye.

She stopped, couldn't believe what she saw at the bar. Maria, Katia, and Nokyung tense beneath the television. Cutters jumped recklessly over waves. A helicopter circled above. The girls began clapping and hollering. Joom missed what they were so excited about because she was focused on the money SevenEight had pulled from his pocket and had folded into Blasko's hand. Then she realized SevenEight saw her and wanted her to know that he saw her. He grabbed his crotch, laughed, and aimed his finger, the shape of a gun. Aimed and shot.

Katia Molino

"Bullshit!" Jimmy Nails leaned over the baize and cornered the three. He worked around the table without looking at the television. "I wished they'd all gone under."

Joom and Maria turned. Joom said, "Be quiet. That's mean."

Katia touched Joom's arm. "Leave him alone."

"But he's—"

"Never mind. Leave him alone."

Katia looked at Maria. Eyes wide, startled. And Joom, too. The skin of her arm was soft and warm. They were the same age. Thrown in with this rough mix who'd skin them alive if given the chance. But who could say? Maria stood bunched in loose clothes with drifting hair shadowing her face. A cute blue band holding up the bangs. A friend of a friend who'd said she was a good worker. And she was. Probably from a squalid hovel in Mexico. Endurance. She had that. To cross the border she'd have to. Katia imagined Maria came with a relative, an uncle, and what he'd put her through to get across. Imagined she'd kept it down. Whatever he'd put her through. Kept it hidden behind those moonless eyes. A friend of a friend, and she got here, in a van reeking of unwashed human flesh.

Jimmy Nails was ranting at the table. "Out for the insurance's what it is. Bullshit!"

On the television the rescuers pulled a man, a woman, and

a small boy from the wreckage. They'd been clinging to a shattered hull and flotation devices. Anything that stayed above water. The woman was in tears. Her face shiny wet, mouth spewing salty water. And crying about her baby. She's still out there! She got away! The announcer cut in. The couple's toddler was still missing. The couple had put the toddler into a large cooler. Tried to hang on. But the waves thrashed them, beat them, and it got away. They could not swim after it. The waves were brutal. Snatched the cooler away. Yanked from the grip. They blinked, and the cooler had disappeared over the top of a distant wave. They were frantic, overwrought with anguish.

"Ain't no fucking baby out there." Nails struck the white ball so hard the crack resounded over the house music. "It's bullshit!"

"Pipe down." Amnaj shouted from across the bar.

"Bullshit!" Nails wasn't looking at the screen. He couldn't see the woman's distraught face. He couldn't see the agony in her eyes. The woman's husband had an arm around her shoulder. He gazed at the ground. His lips grappled one over the other.

"Always an angle." Nails chalked the cue. "Always a scheme. Got Ponzi all over it. Has to be money. You already know it."

Joom's arm slipped from Katia's grasp. Abruptly Joom shouted. "What are you going on about?"

Katia circled her waist, tugged the girl. "Come, come," she whispered in Joom's ear. "Come. Over here, leave it alone."

Nails made his eyes wide. A scary face. He held up the hooks. "Oooo." He laughed.

Joom lurched forward. Katia held her tight. Men who had been sitting at the tables had come to the counter to see the news. One reached out to help hold Joom. Katia waved him off. "Come," she whispered. "Come away."

Joom began to relax in Katia's palms. Then spurred up again. "You don't have no feeling. Don't care for nobody, for nothing!"

Nails raised his head from the shot. "Fuck you."

The men turned. One stepped off a stool. Stance like a hero, he started toward Nails. Amnaj broke around the counter. Stood in front of the man, in front of the others ready to assist the hero. Stood with his arms spread, strong like kegs. A good smile, a thing awake and gentle, working its charm on the crowd.

Katia led Joom to the end of the bar where Castro sat sipping Corona on ice. "Talk to her," Katia said. "Calm her down."

Castro sat upright, flatted a hand across his chest. Blasko, next to him, dozing on the bar.

"Me? Talk to her?"

She glanced at Blasko. "Think he's up to it? Who else?"

"About what?"

"You got brains," Katia said. "Just keep her here."

She returned to Amnaj's side. Saw down his arms, the tender motion of the fingers. He reached across the space toward the men, keeping enough distance to maintain respect. The hushed moment stretched out. A fuse had been lit. Amnaj had stepped in front. He smiled. He blew cool air on the fuse. The men hesitated. In the lull, the Thai ladies arrived and mingled with the men. They giggled like playmates. Seduced and guided the men away from each other, toward tables, beer, girlish talk. Some returned to the counter to hear the news. The rest to their tables.

Nails, behind Amnaj, had the cue ready. He could take them, Katia was certain. Large, and he was swift. She'd seen it before. Badasses calling him out and then hooks or no hooks, one, two, down on the floor.

She snapped at Maria. "Get some drinks around. Apurate!"

A presence behind her. She turned. Amnaj grinning, his eyes amused. "I'm in the wrong business," he said. "I should be a negotiator."

She wiped back her hair. "I'll see if I can find some hostages for you."

Past him to see how Joom was doing and felt his arm brush against hers. He mumbled an apology. She shook her head. "It's nothing."

Castro was deep in monologue. Joom, bored. She wiped drool from the counter, placed a napkin beneath Blasko's mouth.

Katia touched Joom's shoulder. "What's he saying to you?"

"She wanted to know why he's so angry." Castro sipped the beer. "So, I was telling her. You knew he was a boxer, right?"

"Sure."

He looked at Joom.

"A pretty good one, too. Cruiserweight. Had champ written all over him. Went by the name Jack Samsom. And we poured it on. Joltin' Jack, Jammin' Jack. We had a day with him. Real name? Who knows? Nails, Samsom, who knows?

I'm telling you that guy could weather the blows. Couple of concrete blocks for fists. But you never knew with that guy. He'd be pushing fifteen every fight. Down to the final bell, then he'd come on like a bull, all fury and spit, while the other guy was wobbling around the ring. They said he was lucky having that stamina. In control is what I say. That's what he was. Had this fight all lined up for the championship. An easy win, easy. Went up against Arturo Hernandez. Easy money. Easy all the way. And you know they loaded up on him. Easy, easy money. And then Hernandez landed a left in the eighth. They say Samsom took a dive. Someone didn't like that very much and sawed his hands off. They could've let him bleed to death. That would have been humane. But they stanched the wound. They made him live. Wish they hadn't. Sure wish they hadn't."

Katia felt Joom trembling. She frowned at Castro. "This is you trying to calm her down?"

"Much as I like him, you can see it in the face, the eyes, he won't go the distance, he doesn't want to." Castro leaned back. "Best not to be around him."

"A man can be right," Katia said, "and still die. Don't be heartless."

"He does all right, I guess. Got those specially-built devices. Lets him shoot pool, keep his construction job. What more's a guy want?"

"Maybe some dignity."

"Anyway," Castro said. He looked past them, brows arched. He pointed at his chest. Then pointed at Katia. He coughed. "Someone wants you. Maybe you better go."

Katia looked over her shoulder. SevenEight sitting with Dupuis. A crooked finger motioning. She stroked Joom's arm. "You OK?"

She nodded.

"OK, let me go see what this bastard wants."

Neither man rose when she arrived and pulled out a chair and sat with her legs to one side.

"Good to see you again, chiquita." Dupuis extended a hand.

The shine of the silver ring struck her like a smack in the mouth. She looked at SevenEight. It wasn't hard to figure out. Dupuis had gotten her father's ring from SevenEight. Since moving in, he'd taken possession of everything. What favors, she wondered, had it bought him? She balled her hands into fists. Then flattened them against her thighs. She struggled to keep her breath, at once rushing from the lungs, steady and guarded, the way her father had done as a negotiator for the Turbay administration. How proud she'd been. They still told stories of the M-19 rebels taking over the Dominican embassy and the deals her father had made that led to the peaceful release of over sixty hostages. He'd received the ring afterward and before he died had passed it down. It was worth thousands, but she valued it more because of her father's accomplishments. Now it was lodged on Dupuis's finger. A precious silver crown on a tub of shit. She reminded herself to keep cool. Give nothing away.

She ignored Dupuis's extended hand and looked at SevenEight. "What's he doing here?"

SevenEight shook his fingers, looked at Dupuis, and laughed. "Somebody got on her moody boots."

"A real fighter, as I recall." Dupuis's hand sank to the table. Slid it back as if he'd reached out to take a napkin from a dispenser. "And this new one over there. The little yapping Chihuahua. You can see she's a fighter, too. Maybe more than you?"

Katia tracked his target but instead of Maria, she saw Joom loading a tray with beer and shots. "The niece of Amnaj," Katia said. "She's new in country and will leave soon. Nothing to do with Amnaj."

Dupuis forced his fat fingers together. "Speaking of. How's our friend doing?"

SevenEight shook his head. "In deep, man."

"How deep?"

"Asshole deep."

Katia rose from the table. "I need to get back to the bar."

"Not so fast." SevenEight snatched her wrist, pulled her back down. "See at the end there?"

At first, she didn't see anyone. Amnaj and Maria worked behind the counter. The Mexicans clocked up the wall. One drifted over for beer. She shook her head.

"Far end, gray slacks."

"The old guy? You're kidding me!"

SevenEight held her wrist tight. "So, close your eyes, baby. How many fucking times I got to tell you that? He paying real good for this shit. Real good. Just don't let him go falling down the fucking stairs."

The apartment upstairs that Amnaj built so he could be close to the business. He'd told her once that his ex-wife took lovers up there while he was working, so it wouldn't matter if she used it. "It's a haven for whores," he'd said. She knew he'd meant it as a joke on his wife, but it stung bad that he saw her that way.

She laughed. "You are kidding me." Struggled to free her wrist. "He's an old man. He'll die on me. I don't want him to die on me."

"Stand up, baby. Come on. Up, up."

She stared at the old man. He wore a yellow windbreaker with string hanging from it. "This is a fun joke." She looked at Dupuis. He seemed amused. Looked at SevenEight. "A joke, right?"

SevenEight held out some bills. "He been saving up his pussy money, and he ready to cash in. And get this. He asked for you. Don't that fucking beat all? Specificated you, baby."

"It's a joke. Go on, tell me it is."

SevenEight pocketed the cash. Opened a packet of mayonnaise and squirted it on his fingertips. "Stand up, baby. Turn round. He got something special in his dirty old mind. Up, move that ass."

She frowned but rose. SevenEight turned her hips. She felt a hand untucking her shirt. She held still and stared at the old man. Lean with white hair. A cane balanced against his leg. He sipped beer and watched television.

"A little extra," she said. "You got to give me more."

"Sure, baby." SevenEight stood next to her. "Ain't I good to you?"

She felt the hand and the slick chill of the mayo slide down inside the jeans.

"Git now," he said and slapped her ass. "You go on and be a dirty girl."

Amnaj Boonngamanong

He set a beer in front of Reynolds. "On the house." He waited. Reynolds stared at the television, though it was clear that he was staring at nothing. An empty stare into space. "You don't have to put up with it."

Reynolds sat dull-eyed. "That's right." He scooped up the beer. "Don't have to."

He scanned the serving areas. Joom was missing. The air was sweet with sloe gin and citrus. Glasses clinked, ice shifted in the bin. Maria received callouts for beer. Conversations were hive sounds smoothed over with cozy house rhythms. The talk snatches amused him. A couple of men at the bar. Blue shirts, yellow ties. One of them saying, "Our model is the trapezoid." A few minutes later, "It isn't a pyramid. It's more like a spider web." They were laughing, solving important problems. Katia wiped the counter. The girls were in place, except Joom. He searched, but there was Reynolds, in his way, and he'd come to talk to him.

He faced Reynolds. The paralysis in his face. No sense in it. Reynolds, in a bad way. Everyone knew it. But why didn't he stand up? He'd been a soldier. Why didn't he put SevenEight in his place? Made no sense. He couldn't stand to look at him long. Those wasted, unnerving features. A shadow, Reynolds sank below his vision. A slight distraction in the corner of his eye.

Then he rose. There she was. Joom with Blasko near the

food table. What did they have to talk about it? At least she was talking. She wasn't hopeless like her sister. Nokyung at the end of the bar, serving beer to a tall, white haired-man. Nodding when he stuffed a bill into the tip jar. But no smile. Then she cleared a table. A customer approached. Thick-necked and wearing a blazer. He'd been here before. Name-less, like so many. The occasional patron. He stood close, leaned in, put his hand on Nokyung's shoulder. And what'd she do? Stepped away as if he were crawling with lice, so ef-fortless, her evasion seemed natural. Poor girl. Hopeless and plain. She'd never get a man the way she shook them off.

He held Reynolds deep in his gaze, marking off every sin-gle item of his face. "You work in the morning. You look tired."

Reynolds shook him off. "Let me kill it here," he said. "My ride's gone. I'll wait for Katia."

"She'll be late, my friend. Let me get you a taxi."

Dull-eyed and beaten. "I'm good."

He inhaled. A lie, if he'd ever heard one. About to touch the man's shoulder. Buck him up. But Joom went past in a hurry. He knew where she was headed, the angle of the body, purposeful, directional. He watched her go, anger ris-ing with each step. He followed the flight of a napkin to the floor. Does she think I don't know? She stooped at Dupuis's table and swung up toward him, embarrassed and beaming. Oh, she knew how to seduce them. He pressed the counter, felt his hand curl with anger. He yelled, and she looked up. Even in shadows, he saw how her face gathered into a tight point of irritation. What she doesn't know. He waved her on. Then, distracted by shouting. The bar erupted as rescuers pulled bodies from the water. He looked briefly at the television, then at Reynolds. No reaction. Reynolds stared at the television. Stared at nothing. Looked bored. He decided to try again to convince Reynolds to go home, but Joom filled his mind. He strode toward her.

"Didn't I tell you not to go over there?"

"Let go of my arm," she said.

"You disrespect me."

"I dropped something. How can I help that?"

"Don't go over there."

"What do you got against him? You see the money. You see it, don't you? That's my table. And Maria's getting my tips." Her mouth was hard. "My tips."

"I'm not talking about tips."

"Well? What is it?" Then he saw a notion flourish in her eyes. A bright contrast to the obstinacy of the brown cheeks. "Uncle, you're scared of him. That's it, isn't it? You're afraid."

He ushered her to the bar. "You must do as I say, do you understand? You must. You and your sister. You must do what I tell you."

Maria came with ice for the bin. When she looked up, he smiled. She lifted the bucket and dumped it.

Joom glanced at Dupuis. "Uncle, he has money—"

He shook her arm. "Enough!"

Then he saw that she was afraid, too. Excited and afraid. Her worried look helped him relax. He sighed. "Money, yes, but not a husband, ลูก. You are too eager. You don't know that kind of man." He glanced at Nokyung standing quiet and plain and hopeless behind the bar. "And that one. She's like a bride afraid of rain." He sighed again. "You two—was this a mistake?"

Joom wiped her forehead. "What mistake? I am happy to be here."

Reynolds leaned over the bar. He called out over the tumbling ice to Maria. "How about a shot of apple jack, sweetie, and a cold glass of tap?"

"Get back to work," he said to Joom.

She shoved off toward a group of airmen with squared bodies and clean looks.

Reynolds turned. His eyes were dull and his face troubled. "I'm all lost here," he said. "Just wanted to apologize for how I acted. Thanks for the beer."

"It's late, my friend. Think about going home."

"Listen," he said, pausing to toss down the shot. "Talk to Katia for me."

"I'm not getting involved."

"Just talk to her. You're her boss. You can talk to her."

He shook his head.

"You're her boss," he said. Eyes dull. Face weary. "That'll let you stay out of it. Talk to her, will you?"

He stared at the television. Behind him, Nails going on about it. A woman wet from the sea looked distraught. Crying about her baby. A man next to her with an arm around her shoulder. The woman said her baby was lost at sea.

"Will you do it?" Reynolds, the desperate voice.

He blocked out Nails ranting behind him. Shifted to Reynolds. Dull-eyed, a crippled expression. The imploring tone, sickening. He was beaten, helpless, sad. He wanted to help. Wanted to talk to Katia. Do it as a favor. They were such a strange pair. And SevenEight calling him boyfly. Even stranger.

But he shook his head.

"That's your business," he said. "Between you and Katia. You and her. And SevenEight."

Maria Castillo

THE MEXICANS CAME IN around eight o'clock every night. Some, like Maria, were from Jalisco and others from Michoacán or Zacatecas. She enjoyed their familiar accents when they greeted her. Some she did not like, though they came, like Flaco, from her own state. He looked shifty and deranged. Narrow eyes with an obscene luster that unnerved her. He'd catch her eye, and she'd feel her throat constrict, and she would try to hold back the vomit and, unable to, let it drip wet and bitter from mouth to palm.

She hated that Flaco and Joel were cuates. Too close to separate for very long. Joel, a threadbare boy who must have been her age, genuinely seemed to like her. Unlike Flaco, Joel had a friendly smile beneath a fine-sketch mustache and dark eyes and a slanting forehead. She wished he would come to the counter and speak with her, but he stayed with Flaco and the others and took turns shooting pool with Nails.

She tilted a glass beneath the tap and cast an eye at the dark Mexican boy who promised her beauty. Beer foamed in the glass. She placed it and a shot of sour apple and whiskey in front of Reynolds. He paid and tipped her five. She was about to put it in the jar when he grabbed her hand. "For you," he said. She glanced at Amnaj, next to Reynolds, and shook her head. Amnaj waved her off. "Take it." She folded the bill into her jeans.

She wiped the counter to the end and watched Nails line

up a shot, and the Mexicans lined up against the wall. They would come in smelling of rooftops and tar and smile at her and tease while she passed around bottles of beer. They were polite with their hands, but they never tipped, though they looked more grateful than the clean men wearing polos and opening fat wallets. They called her güera. They called her pendeja and mamacita, and they laughed politely, sweetly, to play with her. Especially Joel. He liked to touch her ears when no one was looking. She went by, and he said, "Come away with me, bonita. Come to my room." He grinned at Flaco, next to him, and she felt ashamed that he would share this intimacy with such a repulsive man. She kept her outward appearance light and carefree. But beneath her blouse felt the sweat and summer wind of the Jalisco countryside. She teased. "So, you intend to marry me, with all your money?"

He smiled, playful. "So, you will come?"

"I will not come."

"Room seventeen, chica," he said.

"Room eighteen," Flaco said, "if you want a really big cock."

They howled. She went away, chagrined, heat in her face. But later she would catch his eyes watching her, and she would understand in the way that he raised his brows over the dark eyes that even though he meant only to pry between her thighs and be gone in the morning, he promised it would be very beautiful. Despite her intuition that he would say anything to get her into bed, she could not help imagining that he would please her and that it would be, as he promised, beautiful. And she would forgive him. Instantly. But not the other one. It hurt that Joel stood with Flaco, that they seemed to be friends. Flaco was mean. He was thoughtless and cruel. And she would never forgive him.

Then Katia would catch her flirting and come over to chase her away. "I don't care if you want to be a whore for those boys," she would say. Her tone sharp and bitter. "But they will be rounded up one day, and it will lead to you, and it's back to Mexico."

Katia meant well, but what could she know of her loneliness? She wasn't going to sleep with them. She wanted to be teased by the boy. That was all. Even if it infuriated her at times. The pleasure was worth it. She wanted to be loved. Katia knew nothing of this.

Maria stood next to Joom at the end of the bar. "Anything new?"

Joom turned from the television. "Nothing," she said. "That poor baby. The mother said they thought it would be safe. Putting her in the cooler. She drifted away. How could a mother let go? But she did. Now that poor baby is stranded in a cooler in that horrible sea. Lost in that horrible sea. They search for it, but now they say it cannot survive. The storm is too harsh. That poor baby."

"I have prayed for it," she said. "I have prayed that God will protect it and keep it safe."

"What chance does it have?" Joom said. "They thought they found it. The joy that mother must have felt. All at once. Sweeping, flowing. I know it because that's what I felt. But it was pieces of the boat. Nothing else. All of it washing away."

"All alone out there," she said. "That poor child. I prayed it will be safe. But a prayer doesn't always work."

"They talk about when they will give up the search." Joom opened a package of napkins. "They say it is hopeless."

She sighed and turned away from Joom. Reynolds stared at her. She reversed direction. And then wished she hadn't. He could help, but she was afraid to speak to him. Had been wanting to ask for his help. Too much fear. And now that stare. It pierced the skin, went into the cavity of her chest, and discovered the malice in her heart. She would ask, but it was risky. And hesitated. Not sure about him. Desperation in the eyes. She saw that. The only thing that made him attractive. She believed in desperation. Could count on it. But when she'd turned, he was staring at her. As if he knew already what she wanted.

She helped Joom with the napkins. "I heard what your uncle said about Nokyung. What did he mean?"

Joom laughed a little. "A bride afraid of rain?"

"Yes."

"He means she is a cold fish, afraid of men."

"And he yelled at you."

"You have the good table, Maria."

"You mean the fat man?"

"That's my table." Joom's lips pursed then hardened. "And I have the Mexicans, instead."

"And they never tip."

They fell silent and watched the news. She glanced over her shoulder. Reynolds still staring, but he must have guessed he'd been found out. His eyes shot up at the television. She turned back slowly, hoping to draw his interest.

"Do you think we will find a good man?" she said.

"A nice man with money? I don't know. I had hope when I came here. My uncle said it would be easy."

"Money is good," she said. "But I am afraid because the men play with me."

"It is the nature of the man to play." Joom rubbed her neck. "I hoped it would be different here."

Jimmy Nails called from the pool table. "Joom, get me a beer—that's if you all done taking tea with Maria."

Joom glared at Nails. "I'll trip and throw it in his face," Joom said and tapped out a mug.

She grabbed Joom's hand and laughed. "Maybe he is your money man."

"I'd cut off more than his hands."

She covered her mouth.

Soon as Joom was gone, she went down the bar. Steadied herself on the rail. As she approached Reynolds, she watched the face brighten, the shoulders lifting.

"Maria." His voice quavered. A hand down the arm. Shoulder to elbow. Removing imaginary fluff.

Her fingers shook. She clasped them, set her lips. A loud sound inside her head. A focused thought.

He nodded at the television. "Big storm. They say right at us. The window's wide, though. And that little kid. Think they'll find it? Must be awful for the parents. Can't imagine what they're going through."

She glanced but didn't say anything. He seemed to be studying her, trying to read her thoughts. The longer she waited, the more transparent he became. An inky blot of self-doubt crept over his face. The buildup of desperation. She waited, watched it fill his face with the unbearable sorrow of his soul. She leaned over the counter, fixed herself on elbows, a strong protective stance. Watched the desperation swell in his cheeks, well over into his eyes. She nodded, spoke softly. "Can you get me a gun?" She held his eyes, drove into them. He had to see it inside now.

He leaned back and drummed his chest with nervous fingers. He shook his head. "No, Maria." He looked around, then leaned close. "What do you want with a gun? Someone bothering you?"

"Nothing like that."

"Then what?"

"I live down the road. A small apartment behind a large beach house. A rental cottage, they call it."

"And?"

"It's dark." She glanced around, turned in her shoulders, and made herself seem vulnerable. "And I'm worried."

He rested an arm on the counter. She saw how he worked out what she was up to. Saw it in the crinkled forehead, the expanding lips. His throat rose and fell as he swallowed beer.

"I don't believe you, Maria."

"No?"

"Not at all." He wiped his fingers over his mouth.

She leaned closer, pulled the collar of her shirt out with a finger, as if she were melting, and let the heat simmer in her eyes. "You see how I am."

He nodded. "I see it."

She could tell it took all he had to leave his hand on the counter. Then how his eyes fell on her finger, like a silk insect skating over the skin of his hand.

"I need." She paused and held her lips together and gazed at him. "Your help."

He stretched his neck, shook his head, but he was weak now.

"This isn't smart, Maria. Really, it isn't."

"But."

"But I'll see what I can do."

"Thank you."

"Ray," he said.

"Ray," she said, as if trying to memorize his name.

The way he looked at her. Not reproval, as she first thought. Something else. She sensed she'd been given a fighting chance. That he was glad to give her that.

Someone shouted her name. She spun around. Katia and an old man emerged from the darkness of a hidden stairwell. Katia's hands were in fists. "Maria! Ven aca!"

She rushed over.

Katia fixed her hair into a ponytail. "Why are you talking to him? You're supposed to be working."

"I'm sorry. I had a question."

"I know what you're up to, Maria. I've warned you."

"Maybe he likes me. Why not?"

"¡Qué vergüenza!" Katia said shaking her head. "Do you forget? He's still my husband."

Joom Janpong

"Why the pout?" Nails, pool cue vertical to his body.

Joom set beer on a nearby table and held the tray against her hip. Maria collected money from Dupuis.

"Gotcha," Nails said. "I'm seeing what you're seeing. You're stuck with the Mexicans." He handed her a dollar. "You're stuck with me."

She took the money. "Thanks." Tucked the bill into a pocket. "Yeah, I'm sour. Look at it. Way she walks by, and he's stuffing her pockets. Why shouldn't I be mad? It's my table."

"Smart man, your uncle."

"Smart?"

Dupuis moved and people jumped. SevenEight, especially. Back and forth from the bar to the table. Huge grin. Mouth glinting with gold. Eyes that squirmed and leered.

"A fool, you mean."

"No, baby, I mean smart." Nails pinched the chalk with a hook. "All you see is a bundle of cash on that table and go boo-hooing cuz your uncle won't let you near it. If anyone be a fool here, it be you."

"You starting with me again?"

Nails laughed. "Smart's what I'm saying. Don't you worry none. Your uncle take care of you. Maybe knock you off a little extra. If you can wipe that mean off your face."

"Yeah, between you and them," indicating the Mexicans, "I'll have a Porsche in no time."

Nails chalked the cue. "Don't whack 'em." He went around the table, aimed, and then rose from the stance. "Forget what they look like. They all hungry. They just like your sister. Working hard. Saving money up for the family back home. And the whole lot living in fear of la migra. Know that fear, baby? Bet you do."

Joom chewed her lip. Dupuis and SevenEight were laughing. Looking at her, she realized, and laughing. SevenEight slapped the table. Dipped his head he was laughing so hard. Dupuis shook mounds of fat. The table rocked, their drinks jumped up and down, sloshed over. What was so funny? She felt tricked. They looked and laughed. She clutched the tray to her chest.

A presence near her shoulder. Nails had come around and towered over her. He bent a little, spoke quietly into her ear. "Them wetbacks? They living in fear, baby. La migra coming, like a terminator hound from hell. Gonna sweep 'em right up. Pack them and their taco asses right back across the border. Count on it, baby. Not if. When. But you step back, and give a look. Get your eyeball right on 'em. They still here. Trying to fit in. Not a word of English. And showing up for a little relaxation, and you gonna give 'em the snub? What you got on, baby, some kind of good-smelling shit? I'll tell you something else—"

"I don't want you to tell me something else."

"You ain't gonna get no husband, rich or poor, boom- booming your way through Midsummer."

"Now you're my uncle." She turned and glared. "Stay away from me."

"Maybe I ask my dollar back. You be treating me like that."

She held out the dollar. "Take it."

"Go on." He lined up the shot.

She followed. "Take the dollar."

"Get out of here." He turned his back, focused on the shot. She crumpled the dollar and threw it. It hit his forehead and fell to the floor. His look made her shake with anger. He bent over, clamped the wadded bill between the hooks. Went to the tip jar, eyes on her the whole time, and dropped it inside.

She cried out, air rushing from her chest, and stormed past Nails to the bar, around the counter. Put her hand on her chest and watched it rise and fall. She flew past Maria pouring rounds. Went behind the counter to an area near the staircase and sank into its shadows. The house music flowed over her, and she swayed with it and let its soothing rhythm take hold.

She began to feel better and returned to the counter. Nails worked the table. Unperturbed, as though nothing had happened, as if she hadn't mattered. Cold and unfeeling. Nothing did matter. She didn't matter, and she despised him. The hard flatness of his heart. She wiped a film of sweat from her forehead and set up shot glasses for Maria.

"I wish you took this back," Maria said. "He gives me the creeps."

Dupuis smacked his lips and twirled a fork around his plate.

"He gives good tips. What are you complaining about?"

"Not him," Maria said. "The other one. SevenEight. The way he speaks, the way he looks at me."

SevenEight had put on dark glasses. He seemed to be searching for something. Then a splinter of a smile lit his face. She was his target. He tilted the glasses down, looked right at her.

"Creepy all right." She poured shots for Maria. "But harmless."

Maria wiped spills from the tray. "I heard him talking to Katia about me. They didn't know I could hear."

"Oh?"

Maria arranged the drinks on the tray and lifted it.

"What about?"

Maria looked sick. She held a hand over her mouth, then shook her head.

"What about, Maria?"

A pinched look, as if something rancid had filled her mouth. She shook her head. "I have to go. Get these drinks to them."

Neither warm nor cold, Joom thought, watching Maria slip through the small crowd. Cute but dresses too much like a boy. Smile's too casual. Like she's not trying to make money.

She heard her name. Joel or Flaco. One or the other. They waved. They wanted her. Both looking, both waving. Only Joel smiled. Which had called her name? It was hard to tell.

Nokyung leaned across the bar. "Your table wants drinks," she said, setting her tray on the counter. She looked away. "Amnaj!" She curled her hand, waved him away from Castro. "Three beers. Three buttery nipples."

"You work at the dry cleaners now?" Joom spoke to Nokyung, but she watched Amnaj tap the beer.

"Jit can hire you, too," Nokyung said.

Joom smiled. "That would be good, to earn more money."

Amnaj set a glass down hard on Nokyung's tray. "Maybe you can mind your own business."

Joom faced him. "What business? I can make some money, but you gave away my table."

Nokyung arranged the glasses on the tray. "Don't give away your money so easily."

"Ungrateful nieces. That's what I've got." Amnaj layered the Irish cream. "Why did I bring you? Maybe I send you back. Go on, get to work."

He turned abruptly, went toward Castro.

"I think he's gambling," Nokyung said.

"Of course. You don't know?"

"Ma said he was in a bad crowd once and had many debts."

"He may be forced to sell."

"Is it true?"

"Jing jing. He told me." She wiped wet spots from the counter with a napkin. "He needed money pretty bad. I had to give him some."

"He came to me, too." Nokyung lifted the tray. "I wouldn't give it. It goes to Ma. And I want to leave. So, I save it. It's that bad, really?"

"I don't know. That's what I heard."

The Mexicans cried louder. She got their drinks together while watching Nokyung serve a group of men in dress shirts and loose ties. Slid the tray onto her palm, whisked around the counter. The Mexicans smiled, reaching across, grabbing beer like fish from a cooler. She held the tray out flat, waiting, hoping, but they moved away as soon as they'd snatched the beer, back to the pool table, back to the wall. Nothing but wet stains left on the surface of the tray.

The balls cracked. Nails pocketed the seven off the rail. Lifted his eyes and smiled. She lowered the tray to her thighs. A struggle to keep her face straight and stiff. How she hated this sorry man.

Beyond him, SevenEight rose from Dupuis's table. He dapped the fat man's hand, turned toward the counter, and yelled something to Amnaj, who broke off his conversation with Castro and, without smile or lifted hand, with only the slightest warp of a soft lip, acknowledged that he'd heard SevenEight. He turned back to Castro. The exchange was drowned out by the rustling laughter of the patrons, the deadened clink of glass, the staccato drone of the television, and the apprehensive bass line of the music.

Who else saw it? Joom hoped it was a distortion of light and shadow, a clash of sound and color. When her uncle had turned, had hidden his expression, she'd felt her knees buckle. She hoped it was something else, but she knew it wasn't.

He was terrified.

She took a step to go to him, then stopped. SevenEight made a show of leaving. He made it grand, he made it loud. He pomped out the door and made sure everyone knew it. But that didn't stop her. He went out, and he was gone, and she stopped because Maria dropped her tray on a table. He was gone, and Maria dropped her tray and followed. Long enough, but not too long, and slipped back inside as if she'd never gone out, but the eyes were distant with the burned-out look of someone who'd stared at the sun too long.

Joom caught up with her at the bar.

"You said he was creepy. You said you don't like him."

Maria looked surprised. "I don't."

A quick touch to the arm. "But you followed him. I saw you. Out the door."

"No." Her face deep red. Fingers trembling. "No." Avoiding looks. "I needed air," she said. "That's all."

Nokyung Janpong

The wind picked up the next morning. Steady, dying, rising, dying. The gusts sent trash tumbling down the streets. She drove with the wind. Talk on the radio. Hurricane Molly's speed and direction. The landfall window had narrowed. Midsummer, the likely target.

She rode past the front of Bangkok Cleaners, a yellow brick building with a large, slanted window. The O was missing from the window lettering. A machine parts shop on one side. A real estate office on the other. She parked in back and entered through a narrow door.

Jit instructed her on counter work, the cash register, label and sort items, spot cleaning. "You know how to iron," Jit said. "I'll show you steam press and tunnel finishers later. Get settled right now."

Jit poured cold coffee from a bottle and offered a cup. She declined. Jit switched on a counter television and sat on a cushioned stool.

"How is your mother?"

She smiled. The work felt right. She imagined the amount of money she would save. Saw the outline of the ticket home. The stiff feel of the passport in hand.

"Her health is good. She makes repairs after the floods."

"Ah," Jit said. "The floods are bad. My home in Lampang was swamped. My nephews pitched in to clean up."

She imagined Jit was her mother, and they were sitting on

the porch beneath a mango tree. Just beyond the garden wall, she could hear vendors calling out their wares. Grass jelly coming! They drove small, canopied trucks with loudspeakers. Fresh cabbage! The wet, warm air softened their sound. Soymilk! Durian! She liked the mornings, the stillness, the distant cries, the sleepiness. Her mother sweeping the streets in front of the house.

"She sent me a picture. She is standing knee deep in water in the middle of the street. A look of bewilderment in her eyes."

Jit made a sound and nodded and then scanned the wall, as if watching her own memories.

"Another photo. She is in a canoe. Knees pulled up. She clutches an envelope. A drawstring sack. She presses a golden picture frame against her breast. I recognize the street. A neighbor's spirit house is visible."

Jit sighed. Her eyes drifted to the television. "It is a hard world," Jit said, and she seemed weary, without strength to lift the cup. "Hard and mean."

She was afraid she'd said too much and had brought sadness into Jit's heart.

"Let's work to forget it," Jit said and stood, smiling. She screwed the lid on the coffee bottle. She removed the cups. "Bring a change of clothes tomorrow. It's very hot in the sauna. The steam will drench you. And Gatorade. I have clean laundry to pack. Call if you need me."

She quickly found a rhythm for sorting clothing and inspecting fabrics. With a spotting board, she touched up garments. Compared customer instructions against completed work. Sewed a loose button on a wool cuff. She looked up when vehicles pulled in. A woman with an infant in a front carrier went to the machine parts shop. A man in khaki shorts toward the real estate office.

A black SUV turned in. She took interest when no one emerged. A sweater lay across her lap. She dabbed a resistant stain with a white cloth. Then a man climbed out. Curious and guessing whether real estate or machinery was his destination. He stripped dark glasses from his face and pushed inside, closing the door quietly against the wind. She set the sweater aside, stood ready at the counter. His face turned slightly red, a smile drawn up suddenly, as if he'd been surprised.

"You don't remember me," he said and thrust out a ticket.

She examined his face. Hard ears, thin lips, illusive eyes. A rule-bender with authority. Instantly, felt her face turn sour. Shook her head and took the ticket.

"En La Playa," he said. "Last night. I was with Reynolds."

A band of gold on his finger. He must have noticed she was staring and slipped his hand below the counter. When the hand emerged, the ring was gone. A faded circle of depressed skin remained.

"I don't remember." She looked at the ticket.

"My first time there."

She shrugged and went to retrieve the items. A cluster of plastic-wrapped coats matched the number on the ticket, and she brought those out. Rematched the tickets and held up the coats. He slid his fingers under the hanger hooks.

"Some news, isn't it?" he said, a glance at the television.

"Storm's coming faster than predicted. Too bad for the Cooler Baby. Drowned already, I suspect. They'll give up the search soon enough. A matter of time."

"I hope not."

"I'm Derek Stickleback."

He had the coats and had paid. Certainly, he knew that they were done. He seemed to be trying not to look at her. She felt uncomfortable and wished he'd leave. She nodded.

"Lieutenant with the sheriff's office."

"Nokyung."

"I know. Reynolds told me last night."

"Oh."

"Interesting place. How'd you get there?"

"My uncle is owner."

"I see." He dangled the coats down his back. "Interesting people."

She shrugged, lifted herself onto the stool she had been sitting on, and bunched the sweater in her lap. "I have work to do."

"In my business," he said, chuckling, "maybe I should be checking for green cards, you think?"

She dabbed solvent on a white cloth. "Is it your business?"

"No. Sorry. Just a joke, OK? Just kidding."

She turned toward the television. "You make joke on me."

"Right. Guess it's not funny."

She stared at the television, touched the white cloth to the sweater, and imagined that he had gone from the shop. That he had left a gray residue, a smudge of himself, against her eye. That this was the lingering shadow that encroached from across the counter. Without looking, she recalled his face. Prudent jaw lines. A relaxed mouth that avoided reaction. In the quickness of his eyes, she saw that nothing got past him. And there on the counter, the hand lying curled like a sleeping animal and the wedding ring. He wore it, he slipped it off, made himself what he is not. The face of a deer, the heart of a tiger.

"Yep," he said. "That storm's coming for us. I don't think they'll find it."

Startled at the sound of his voice, she hunched forward, kept silent. Refused to speak. Glanced at the television. A commercial break. The sound of shoes moving away. She watched her fingers work on the sweater. The door opened. A wave of warm wind flowed over her face. A tingling sensation rising from her skin. She looked up. He was hanging the coats in the SUV. Powerlines swayed. A plastic bag dashed into the street. It came to a halt and lay there panting. She could read on the bag Dixie each time the wind inflated it. Then, as if struck by a sense of purpose, the bag jumped up and scrambled to the other side of the street. She began to laugh and did not see him at the door. He strode to the counter.

"Would you care for a drink?"

She stared. Unsure if he meant her. But who else? They were alone.

"I am not thirsty."

He smiled. "I meant later. After work."

The white-lined finger flat on the counter. She shook her head.

"I go to the bar when I am done here."

"That's right. Maybe another time?"

"Maybe not."

She watched his lip turn up. Curled fingers on the counter, drawn slowly away. He left without looking back.

She phoned Joom. "We need to get bottled water and batteries this afternoon."

Banners at the store across the street flapped briskly.

"I'll pick you up at four."

She felt the warmth of the steamers in the back.

"OK. Five."

She slipped the phone into her back pocket.

A flurry of wind tossed the world outside, and this was just the beginning. Surrounded by the sticky heat, she felt numb but also strangely attracted to the fury of the storm. Beyond sight, it raged black and violent, and she sensed that she belonged to it.

Ray Reynolds

Corporal Ray Reynolds sat in his cruiser beneath a sprawling oak on the edge of a nearly empty shopping center. Light rain danced on the windshield. He looked around, relieved that few other cars were nearby. It'd been a nasty day already, and this was one more thing to do. He'd already attended hurricane preparedness at the emergency operations center. Then he'd met Maria at a convenience store.

Slipping the snub .38 from the armory was easy enough. Heebner had been on duty. He was a distracted mess, ever since he'd nearly shot his own man in a confusing, dark warehouse. Really rattled the guy. He got a desk during the investigation, and then even after he was cleared, he seemed to need it. Couldn't blame him.

Reynolds palmed the swipe card from Heebner's desk, got the passcode from a sticky posted on the side of the monitor. He had the revolver in his pocket when Heebner rounded the corner, a nervous smile etched over his face. Reynolds made himself relax, smiled, easy does it.

"What's new, Erik?"

"You hear?"

"Not a thing."

"I'm back on the street tomorrow." Heebner held his breath, which made the shaky smile on his lips expand into thick strips of whitish-pink.

"Congratulations. You ready?"

Heebner shrugged. "Guess I better be."

Reynolds, hand in pocket, over gun, closed the door. In, out. And no one would miss it.

Hadn't really thought it through last night when he'd said he'd get it for her. Hoped she was just talking and hadn't meant it. But she'd come up as he was leaving and had grim eyes and didn't say a thing. But he knew. She sought a sign of sincerity. Her eyes had searched his face, and he'd had to look away. What he'd seen was frightening. She grasped his arm, his shirt, tugged him back. Hadn't said a thing. Just that look. And he knew she meant it.

Her request lingered in his mind long after he'd gone home. He woke up with her voice in his head. A simple, childlike tone. "Can you get it?" And when it became clear that he would, he didn't hesitate.

He told her he'd wait at the convenience store fifteen minutes. No more. And had barely pulled in when she came up fresh and breezy. He'd never seen her in daylight. Her hair flowed over her shoulders in the drizzle of the gray morning. She stood with her hands hidden in a jacket at the open window. Head barely reached the top of the cruiser. He handed over the paper bag like it was a sack of brownies. She said something about his uniform, about it making him look majestic. He chuckled at the word choice. She stared at him.

"I'm not laughing at you," he said.

The wind streaked her face with hair. An impulse to ask her to sit with him in the vehicle. He imagined what she would look like next to him. He'd take her somewhere. Saw how the road was long, barren, and warm. A destination too far off to be known.

"Like I said last night," he said. "This is not smart. Not a good idea."

She swayed in the breeze, hands shoved in pockets, lips closed and inexpressive.

"It's unloaded," he said. "Shells are your problem."

She nodded. Hair flowed across the face.

"If you need something," he said, though he didn't know why he'd said it.

She pulled a hand from her pocket and raked the hair away.

"Thank you," she said. A smile surfaced.

"You've got a pretty smile," he said.

"Why?"

He hadn't known what to say. What was the answer? Then something tenacious in her eyes. Suspicion, vigilance, fear. But no invitation to pry.

"Good-bye." He put the car in reverse.

In the mirror, just before he'd turned onto the main drag, he watched her vanish around the corner, gone the way she had come, in silence and obscurity.

•

HE WAS TIRED OF waiting. Scanned the parking lot. Where the fuck was he? Felt restless. Needed to keep moving. Four years had gone by. Just like that. The smell of camels still tainted the skin no matter how much he washed. He'd barely come up for air when he'd been hired by the sheriff's office, thanks to Stickleback, and this was no better than grunt work.

Only a perversion of hope strung him along. A dark night down an alley. A bullet meant for him.

Katia had tried to understand. He gave her that. But saw it was hopeless the moment he stepped off the plane. She'd rushed to him in the terminal, face wet with tears, face bright, happy that he was home. Home and safe. She'd thrown her arms around him. A convincing clutch that promised she'd never let him go. Had she noticed? How he'd stood there, throwing off no more warmth than a roll of C-wire? He still saw it plainly. He was supposed to feel elated, joyful, and happy. He should have expanded around her, engulfed her with his own delight at seeing her and holding her after so long. Should have felt the heart beat faster. Instead he let her hug him while he stared at a kiosk selling tourist T-shirts.

He'd never fired his gun on duty. Not once since Afghanistan. He hoped for the bullet everyone avoided. The one that was spoken of as Destiny, Fate. The one with your name on it. But it never came. He wasn't afraid. He sought it. But it never came. He couldn't do it himself. Put the barrel of his Beretta in his mouth. Something, not hope, stopped him. He envisioned a random executioner. A nameless entity taking him by surprise. Darkness would shroud the assassin. Had to be that way to bring out the necessary fear. The certainty that he would be powerless when the time came. The humiliation of being destroyed without dignity. Helpless and disabled by terror. And then death at the last possible moment. Down every barrel he searched for the fatal bullet.

The bullet never arrived. But SevenEight did. A phone call from an unknown number. He answered and knew instantly he could never resume his life. SevenEight knew his habits and at first supplied him and then drained him. This, too, fit the damnation he deserved. He accepted the role without question.

SevenEight had been a hero, a chest of medals. One stood out more than the others. One had saved his life. A cloudless, windless day at the observation post. A recent rain had kept down the moon dust. Wolford was sitting next to him, praying for a firefight. They all were. It had been weeks, and boredom was making them crazy. He was carving a section of packing foam into flip-flops. Next to him, Bell was breaking down the SAW for the millionth time. SevenEight and the Mackies were demonstrating chokeholds on the cherries. All in good fun. Turner encouraged them from where he was standing at a piss tube. Always someone jacking off in the B-huts, one dull moment to the next. What made it worse was intel that there was movement among the mountain shale. But no contact. They were itchy for contact and becoming loopy with boredom.

Reynolds walked over to Turner. Then Turner exploded. He heard snaps and felt something like a hammer whacking his leg. He went down. The OP was getting rocked. RPGs exploded near bunkers. In shorts and bare feet, Wolford ran past with a grenade launcher. Reynolds felt lightheaded. Thought he was bleeding out. He was wet all over and realized after a moment it was Turner. His liver and shit. Someone shouted that they were being overrun. He couldn't move and began yelling and stared at the sky. RPGs threw up dust. Gunfire, uneven and unsettling, like roofers doing double time. A shadow passed over.

SevenEight and Sgt. Dunfee returned fire. SevenEight knelt down. Packed Keflex into his leg, told him he was all right. Then he was gone. Warthogs in the sky. Dust in the nose. The scuffle of confused boots. The whistle of RPGs. Turner's guts soaked into his skin. He shivered, as if packed in ice.

He found out later what happened. Gramps and Slater were outside in a bunker. Guns were jamming. They were tossing hand grenades and running back. Gramps got hit in the leg. A bullet pierced Slater's shoulder, ricocheted, and came out his groin. They were being dragged away into sagebrush. SevenEight scrambled after them, taking out their captors with quick, deadly shots. Apache rockets lit up fixed positions. Chain guns ran the squirters back into the mountains.

Reynolds closed his eyes. An image of SevenEight kneeling beside him. Didn't remember anything after that. Hated being there. But when he was away, he couldn't wait to get back. It gnawed at him. His buddies were fighting, they were dying, and he couldn't get back soon enough.

He returned two weeks later. How close he'd come, he told SevenEight, and cried on his shoulder. Don't be a pussy, SevenEight said but held him. Don't be a fucking pussy. He stuck to SevenEight. He was lucky, brave, had saved lives.

SevenEight took him in. And things began to change between them.

He knew then he'd lost his place. Knew it and didn't mind. Did what he was told because he was afraid. Deep down-to-the-bone afraid. Couldn't get past the fear. Until the next firefight. He thrived on adrenaline. Between times, he was filled with nagging predictions. He would never see Katia again. He would die in the dust. He would explode like Turner and become a dark liquid seeping forever into the Afghan soil.

Outside a firefight, SevenEight was the only relief from fear. The squad was a bond of death. He would die for them, they would die for him. Every man in the squad, without saying so, knew it. Something else with SevenEight. The image that he was not going to die. He devoted himself to that image. Then he didn't die. And Katia no longer inspired him.

What are you, a fucking pussy? SevenEight said. Reynolds didn't mind. If he could stick with SevenEight, he would be all right. He told SevenEight of the fear. He told him everything. You're a fucking pussy, SevenEight said. But he didn't mind because he was taken in, and he believed he would get out alive, and later when they kicked down the door in the no-go zone of Panjwai, he kicked hard because SevenEight said so. The family had been sleeping. The parents in one room, the girls in another. The gray-bearded grandfather on a cot. SevenEight said to cut their throats. The others jumped on it, but he hesitated. A fucking pussy, SevenEight said, and the others laughed, and while they joked and laughed with blood flooding from the throats of the family, he felt ashamed. The shame filled his body. His focus narrowed. It burned. He lifted the head of the youngest girl and cut her throat. He watched the outflow of hot blood on his hands. He looked at SevenEight. He wanted approval. He looked at the others. They were laughing. He looked at SevenEight. The scorn in his eyes. He felt his body softening, pleading, begging for recognition. SevenEight shook his head and turned away. Goddamn fucking pussy. SevenEight, with a dismissive laugh. A rejection sharper than the blade in the wet crimson hand. The girl's taut, black hair curled around his fingers. He felt as if he might cry because SevenEight had spurned him. And then he did cry. The girl's head swayed under the hand. SevenEight said, Fucking pussy, and spat on him as he went past. The others spat on him as they went past. His eyes stung. He looked at the girl's head hanging from his hand. He felt redeemed. And he was still alive. And swarmed with a sensation he'd never felt. More than gratitude, more than adoration. He scrambled after SevenEight, loving him as he'd loved no other. After that, he deleted email from Katia. She was junk mail. Along with his parents, his brother, his friends. Within that insular group, he'd found his place.

When he returned to the States, he had to stay busy. Katia begged, Stay home. He couldn't. Not after what had happened. The atrocity of the deeds haunted him. It made the soul thin and atrophied. Breathing unbearable.

He was different now. A depleted stranger. She lit candles, made dinner, adored him. It didn't matter. The sight of her disgusted him. The smell of her hair, the sound of her voice. Her dark fingers on his neck. He nearly broke them. It wasn't her fault. Katia had nothing to do with it.

But he shoved her away and felt lost once more. And began to search for the bullet. He needed the edge, the sizz of danger. He took the deadly assignments and searched for it. Death eluded him, and then, worse than death, the call one night in October.

A month later, SevenEight moved in.

•

Reynolds jerked at the hard rapping on the window. Felt detached from himself. Unhinged and numb and distant. And watched the finger as if it were someone else's pressing the button that unlocked the door. SevenEight slid into the cruiser. Beyond him, a red car came to a stop in the parking lot.

"Goddamn," SevenEight said and lit a cigarette. "Was just thinking about that time we took contact. That time Gramps got his fucking arm shot off."

"Don't smoke in the vehicle."

SevenEight inhaled and blew smoke in Reynolds's face. "Crack the fucking window, will you?"

Reynolds turned the key and cracked the window.

"Brrrp, brrrp." SevenEight held his arms up in a firing position. "Brrrp. Hajj points all over the place, remember that? And Dunfee's always telling us to shut the fuck up. What'd he say? What was that, y'all—hick-stick from Ken-tuck-y. Cousin-fucking bastard from Ken-tuck-y—y'all, y'all quit that horse-assin' around. That what the nigger say. Shit."

Reynolds stared out the window. The oaks were heavy with acorns. A breeze shook them off.

"I've got work to do. What do you want?"

SevenEight blew smoke through the crack. "That was some day. Some motherfuckin' day. Gramps on flank bitchin' about insufficient military pussy, remember that? And we just strolling along, and them fucking AKs start pissing on us, and we got the goddamn low crawl going on for positions. But not Gramps. He just stand there all cool like Cornelius and stretch down and pick up this thing look like a goddamn sausage roll.

And nature freak Frankie Bell go to screaming, 'It's his fucking arm, it's his fucking arm,' and we using brass hard on hajj, and here come Gramps carrying the shot-off arm down the middle of the road like he in some fucking zombie movie."

SevenEight sucked deep and laughed and blew the smoke out the crack. "God damn that was some motherfucking day."

Reynolds stared out the window. The oaks were fat and swayed in the wind. Beyond them, vehicles glided soundlessly over the street.

He remembered. He remembered when Frankie Bell was shot in the mouth. He remembered Wolford falling like a pane of glass. He remembered Ritchie Rich, a cherry three weeks in from Plano, clutching his guts in his lap after an RPG slammed through the B-hut he was sleeping in. He remembered Slater the Magician who never came back from leave. They'd heard later he'd been bludgeoned during a bar fight. He remembered Turner exploding into a chunky stew all over him. And McPhearson. Shot in the head. Fell off a cliff. All at once. They called him Mackie-Two because McWhorter already went by Mackie. So, Mackie-One and Mackie-Two. The Mackies if you were talking to both. And then Gramps. He was twenty-seven and prematurely gray. His arm got shot off, and he picked it up and walked down the street like he was already dead and nothing could hurt him. He remembered. Every detail, every sound, every smell. Even the taste of the moon dust like a mouthful of dirty hair. Time had stopped. It now hovered and saturated him like a dark storm.

"So, hear up," SevenEight said. "Gonna take care of some things. What, don't concern you."

Reynolds stared out the window. Rain fell harder and turned the oaks and the traveling vehicles into runny smears. Stiffness grabbed his jaw and neck. A coil of anger, infinitely small, packed tight in his throat. It would not release. For three years, SevenEight had torn him down, put him in debt, and held out redemption by involving him in illicit activities. And then when he'd maxed out, SevenEight demanded payment. Now that he was in deep, now that he had no money, no hold on his dignity, he wanted it all back. SevenEight thrust Panjwai like a gun to his head. He'd fucked Katia and then put her to work. You owe me, he'd said, and put Katia to work. He had nothing to cling to. The coil of anger would not release.

"Hey, buzzkill," SevenEight said, poking him in the arm. "Wake up over there. Look like you're thinking. You thinking? You don't need to think."

Reynolds stared out the window. "Yeah," he said, "I was thinking."

"Well, stop it. And listen up."

"Was thinking, why we weren't good soldiers."

"Cuz we the shits at the bottom of the shit burner, man. Now, you stop all that, and get your ass back to now."

SevenEight flicked the cigarette through the crack.

"Tomorrow night. You and I are at International."

"The pool hall."

"Right."

"Your alibi."

"We're there. That's what you need to know. You're there. I'm there. We been there the whole fucking night talking about the fucking war. Shit like that, whatever. You look like you're thinking. Stop thinking."

"Yeah." Reynolds turned. He looked at SevenEight and then stared out the window. "Yeah, I was thinking. I was thinking, you know, I've never killed anyone since I got back, but sometimes I dream all day long about taking this gun from my holster and shoving it up your ass and pulling the trigger until all the bullets are gone, and you're up there singing opera with bullets flying out your mouth. That's what I was thinking."

"What's all this? I got me an uppity bitch?" SevenEight began to laugh. "That what I got, ain't it? Shit. A fucking uppity bitch."

He laughed, and Reynolds stared out the window, but then he began to laugh, too. Couldn't stop himself. The laughter was weak and mixed with sadness, but he laughed, and SevenEight laughed, and they were both laughing. SevenEight's laughter was hard and derisive. Reynolds burned with shame and realized he had stopped laughing and that the sound was now a soft whimper.

SevenEight snapped, and he flinched.

"Got them sniffles again, boyfly," SevenEight said. "You do got that thing for crying, ain't you? Well, I ain't gonna hurt you."

SevenEight slapped him hard.

Reynolds felt blood rush to his eyes. He looked down. His hands were shaking.

"Don't try to think, boyfly," SevenEight said. "That shit be my worry. Ain't I take good care of you? Come on, now, like in the B-hut."

He felt SevenEight's hand on the back of his neck. He was wiped out. It would never stop. The hand tugged. Little nudges downward.

"Come on, now." SevenEight unzipped his pants. "Make the nigger smile. Sing me some opera on the McJuicy."

He felt the nudges, the dull, prodding fingers.

"You're a sick man, Reynolds," SevenEight said. "Need you some therapy help or something. Don't fool me none. Not one minute. I seen that smile on your face. I seen it. That sick smile when you cut that girl's throat."

He didn't know he'd smiled until SevenEight had said it. Hadn't known. But he must have smiled. He must be sick. SevenEight had said he'd smiled when he'd cut her throat. He must be sick. All payback, this, too, and the bullet that tortured him by avoiding and letting him live.

The last thing he saw before he closed his eyes and opened his mouth was the red car in the parking lot and the familiar, uncomprehending face behind the wheel.

Maria Castillo

Maria lugged a case of bottled water into her cottage through the slashing rain. She emptied the contents of a plastic bag onto the kitchen table: a flashlight, batteries, a box of pads, a frozen entrée. She looked at the clock. Three hours before work, and enough time for a nap and a shower. She turned on the television and fell across the couch with her feet tucked under her thighs. The rain beat in loud and soft rhythms, alternating its tempo like a spirited mariachi against the concrete blocks of the cottage.

On the small screen, helicopters flew over the Gulf of Mexico, gray like the sky and indistinct, as if there were no difference between them.

The water was empty.

She prayed for the Cooler Baby, afraid they would never find it. She glanced at the statuette of Guadalupe on the altar she'd made from driftwood. Surrounding it, silk roses, a retablo of Jesus and Mother Mary, and an empty soda bottle found on the beach and kept because she'd seen in it an angelic reflection.

Near the altar, gold-framed photos of her parents, grandmother, and two younger brothers. She missed them, especially her mother, who told her to go, while her father resisted. Somehow her mother had known it was best. Her brothers each secretly told her that they hoped she would send for them first. Her grandmother, against her beliefs, took her into town and purchased birth control pills. She gave her a pewter milagro of a woman's leg and tied the chain around her neck. "It will keep you safe on your journey," she said.

She muted the television, the sound of the helicopters. She feared the sound and had begun to tremble. The horrible sound of the helicopters. The Lizard had called them moscas—desert flies. She pulled a woolen blanket over her legs and thought of Joel. He would not be working on a day like this. She imagined that he was next to her. She traced the peach fuzz over his lips with her finger. She heard him say softly, Come away, bonita, come to my room. And she saw herself rising from the couch and being led into the bedroom. She glanced at the Mother of God and saw that her beautiful face had become a scowl, and her tender hands scolded from the blue robes. A flicker from the television, the gray endless sea. She prayed to remind herself that she was pure and good.

A colored map of the search area. The storm now fully sitting in the Gulf and its path constant, as if nothing could sway its course. She searched for the English word. A beeline toward Midsummer. It came like wrath, she thought. "It comes for me," in a whisper.

A helicopter crossed the screen, and though the sound was muted, she still heard the blades snapping in the sky above her. She closed her eyes and saw the sea become the desert. Waves of heat, emptiness, desolation. Terror and pain. The journey had begun with her uncle.

•

HER FATHER'S BROTHER HAD a friend in Mexico City who knew a coyote who could smuggle her into the United States.

She traveled from Jalisco by bus and found the coyote in Nogales. He was called The Lizard. His clothes were dirty and stained with sweat. She avoided the stare of his black eyes. He locked her hand within his and caressed her wrist and took her money. She was led to a guest house in Sasabe. A windowless room with seven others, all men. The room was bare except for a decrepit cot. She had heard that she should pair up with someone for protection. She sat on the dirt floor with her back against the wall and gazed at the men. An old man sat on the cot with two others. He had gray stubble and seemed to have no business being in the room. She believed he would not make it.

Next to him, the two men spoke in whispers to each other. The loose similar way they moved their hands and licked their lips made her guess they were brothers. The rest sat aloof and alone, bundles of stinking, sour flesh crouched or stretched on the floor.

A young man caught her attention. He wore denim with frayed cuffs. A straw hat obscured his face, but she was still able to make out the candid shape of his mouth. He had long, thin fingers that rested delicately on the tops of his boots. She decided that he was the one who would have compassion for her.

She pulled her hair back, wiped sweat from her neck with a bandana, and closed her eyes. Except for the whispering brothers, there was no other sound. They waited in the stifling, sour heat for several hours. Time had disappeared, could no longer be measured by clocks or breath.

The Lizard pulled open the door and led them to a muddy

minivan. The sky was bronze. A warm late afternoon wind felt refreshing after the long confinement. The Lizard drove them into the desert. His voice slashed the quiet of the afternoon. He told them it was a day's journey. He told them they must follow his direction, or he would abandon them. He told them there were bandits, and he could not guarantee anything. "Don't get sick," he said. "Don't fall behind, don't wander off, and don't piss unless I tell you—or you will be left behind. You are to do exactly as I say."

She carried two one-gallon jugs of water that strained her arms with their weight and shouldered a brown backpack her father had given her. They set off in single file. The sun slithered down the back of a distant mountain range. Someone said, "It's Christmas day." A few chuckled, then they lapsed into silence. The only sound was the cadent crunch of boots on the rocky soil.

Coyotes howled in the distance. She shivered as the air temperature began to drop. Shivered because the coyotes howled long and loud. Shivered because their laments became something else, something attached to her fear.

She struggled to remove her jacket from her backpack and keep up with the column. The man with the long, delicate fingers plucked the jacket out and gave it to her. She smiled, though she knew he could not see her face in the darkness, and felt relief. She'd been right to pick him. Hope flourished like a cactus flower in her breast. They tramped along in silence beneath a blossom of stars.

His name was Otilio. He was from Zacatecas. A photo he carried showed a wife with a blush of pink in her cheeks and a daughter with a single tooth framed by round and amazed lips. Otilio studied mathematics but had no money and intended to earn enough to go to the university when he returned home. Sometimes he stumbled on the trail, and she caught him, and they would laugh quietly. They crossed ravines that sent them sliding down into darkness and dust. A shape in front blocked the sky. "The Baboquivari Mountains," Otilio said. Then he leaned into her as they trudged up an incline. "Cold. Very, very cold." A moment later, he said, quietly and with a shiver in his voice, "I don't think it will be a day as The Lizard says. I calculated the distance before we left." Otilio limped, and at times, his breath became shallow or heavy. A struggle to keep air. "What's wrong?" she said. "Thorns," he said. "A cholla cactus or prickly pear. The pain is eating through my foot." "You must stop," she said. "No," he said. She reached for his hand, found that it was balled into a fist, and she could not loosen it. "How far?" she asked. "Four days, no less." He pushed ahead with a grunt, and she doubled the pace to keep up.

The Lizard said they would stop and rest. A creamy, pink sun rose over the landscape. They hid under bushes and curled up with their backpacks. She sat on a stony ledge and watched the sun climb higher. She felt a chill and turned. The Lizard was standing behind her. He came around and squatted. He drilled a small hole with his finger in the dirt at her feet. "A sunrise on the desert is pretty," he said, "but nothing compared to you, nena, don't you think?" She looked away from the black, narrow eyes and set her jaw tight. He drew a long cactus shape between her feet. "The price of admission," he said, and touched her leg. She moved her foot over the shape, erasing it. "I've paid you," she said. "You took the money." He chuckled, then sighed. "But I have counted, and it is not enough." "I counted it, too, and it was enough." "No," he said and rose to his feet. "You will pay, or you will not make it. Get some sleep. We have a long way to go."

She curled up in the dirt near Otilio. He turned and looked at her. Her head on the backpack. "He says he wants more," she said. He sighed. "What can you do?" She looked at him until his face became smeary from the water in her eyes. She closed them, so he would not see. Not long after, she felt a boot on her backside. She looked up. The Lizard stood over her. "Vámonos," he said.

She rose to an elbow and wiped sweat from her face. Swished water to remove the bready taste of sleep in her mouth. Otilio lay next to her. He didn't appear to be breathing. She shook him several times before he turned. His face had become pale, and rings of red diminished the size of his eyes. "You're not OK," she said. "I'm OK," he said, but he lay there, his wan face like a Día de los Muertos mask. She heard The Lizard yelling and looked up. The old man had poured water on his bandana to wipe his face. "Goddamn you." The Lizard had the old man by the collar. "You're wasting the water, and you will die out here." He turned to the brothers who were shouldering their packs. Turned to the others and glared. "All of you, listen up. Drink the water. Don't waste it. If you need to moisten your face, piss on it. Now, let's go."

The climbs were treacherous, the downhills slippery. One of the brothers tumbled down a ravine and banged up against a rock. His brother scooted after him, helped him up, but no one else stopped. She found a steady rhythm that eased the pain of blisters on her feet. The rhythm detached her from her body. Her mind floated over the rocky soil. She gazed hypnotically at a distant plateau, and beyond that, a flat desert filled with mesquite and chaparral. Otilio limped behind, one foot dragging over the ground. His eyes were cast upward, as if he were traveling toward the clouds or nowhere in particular. At the bottom, when the land began to spread out into a sea of red soil, they stopped. The Lizard called them all together. He pointed at a pair of high-top sneakers, one of them with a leg bone protruding from it. He pointed and said nothing. He pointed a long time. He pointed and stared at each of them. He pointed and looked at her. He smiled when he looked at her. She understood that he was showing her that death was real and that she had not paid enough. They marched on through the hot red mouth of the desert.

They camped in the afternoon. "A few hours," The Lizard said, "and then we go through the night."

She pulled thorns from her ankles. The skin bled, but relief was instant. Some thorns were tricky and caught her fingers, and they bled. The Lizard crouched beside her. "Not like that." He lifted a comb from his pocket and held up her ankle. "This way." He ran the comb over her skin. The thorns came out in clumps on the teeth of the comb. "Keep it," he said, handing her the comb. "I have plenty." He went away, and she turned to Otilio, who was already asleep. She lifted his pants leg. His ankles were covered with thorns. She brushed the comb over his skin. He did not wake up.

The Lizard shook them from a thin sleep. Darkness had fallen. The coyotes were howling. She shivered and clutched her jacket tight around her shoulders. The chill got in anyway and scraped its icy nails along her skin. Her teeth felt gritty. She swept the taste from her mouth with her fingers. She was out of water. Everyone was out of water. The Lizard said they would find cattle ponds and refill. She hitched up her pack and shook Otilio. He was heavy and stiff and dead. The moment she touched him, she knew that his journey had ended. She took the photo of his wife and daughter from his pocket and put it in her pack. He was from Zacatecas. That's all she knew.

"We can't leave him here," she said to The Lizard.

"Stay if you like," he said. "Bury him if you like. Everyone else, come on." And he went down the path.

Everyone followed. She glanced over her shoulder at Otilio. She'd neglected to pull his pants legs back over his calves. She paused, as if she might go back. Then hustled to catch the column marching across the desert.

They came to a simple barbed-wire fence. The Lizard greeted them as they crossed, "Welcome to America." She looked back at Mexico, as if she expected she would be lifted in spirit by the crossing, but she felt nothing, or she felt the same. As if, in truth, nothing important had happened. She hefted the backpack and footslogged across the desert. Otilio had told her that when they crossed, they would be in the Tohono O'odham Reservation in southern Arizona where The Lizard had contacts. From there, they would travel Interstate 19 to a safe house in Tucson. Her arms and legs felt as if knives had been driven into them. The pond water she had remaining was speckled green with grit and feces. She twisted the dusty cap and drank it.

In the afternoon, when the heat bore down like fire and their feet hurt from the hot gravel and sand of the desert, The Lizard began shouting. Maria had been watching her feet. Amazed by how they moved like pendulums, forward and back, forward and back. Her mind had emptied itself of all thought. Nothing but the one, single motion of stepping. The numbness and exhaustion.

The Lizard ran through the column shouting, "Moscas! Moscas! Run for the bushes!" The line stopped, and no one moved. They stood like thickheaded cactus hypnotized by the thump-thump-thump-thump. The Lizard shouted, "Moscas! Moscas! Run! Hide!" And then they saw the helicopter. The sound of its blades shot into her ears and chopped through the nerves of her body. It swooped low and sizzled as it went past. The distorted sound of her heart seemed to be beating on the outside of her chest. The old man hobbled off the trail. She ran after him. The brothers scampered into a thicket of mesquite. The Lizard shouted, "Hide the jugs! Hide the water!" She remembered that he'd said the jugs were easy to spot from the air. She found the old man flat on the ground in a cluster of chaparral. She dove next to him and laid her jacket over the water. The helicopter circled back, came lower, and swept sand and rock into their faces. She covered her ears and began to pray out loud. She heard the old man praying out loud. The helicopter fried the air above them. It hovered a moment longer before setting out, before it was nothing but a distant murmur. And then the desert snapped silent once more.

They came to a dirt road, and The Lizard said they would camp. He moved them out of sight of the road and passed around Ramen noodles, which they ate cold. The light began to fade into evening. She couldn't eat the noodles and gave the remaining clump to the old man. The two brothers sat across from her and whispered. The old man, who'd never said a word during the entire trip, sipped from a jug. The Lizard stood and looked at her. He stood behind her. She looked at the men. They did not look back. They did not look at The Lizard standing behind her. They stared at the ground. They stared as if they were already asleep. The old man next to her slowly munched on the noodles she had given him, and he stared at the ground and chewed like a slow, dull beast.

"Levántate," The Lizard said. "Ven conmigo."

She looked at the men and hoped that The Lizard was speaking to one of them. They didn't look back. They stared at the ground. She felt a knee in her back, nudging her forward. A knee forcing her toward the ground. Forward, she bent to relieve the pressure of the knee and then struggled to her feet. The Lizard locked her hand and led her away. She cried back to the men. They stared at the ground. The Lizard strode swiftly through the bushes, along the desert sand. Yanked her through the darkness. She cried and tried to pull away, swatted at him. She stumbled and swayed. As if she were weightless, as if she were nothing, he dragged her through the brush. Then he stopped, yanked her up, and punched her in the stomach. Dropped to her knee. A punch in the mouth. She fell to the ground, fell on sharp rocks and thorns and lost her breath. After that, it was easy. A sharp knee between her thighs. The milagro of the woman's leg ripped from her throat with a brittle snap. The milagro her grandmother had given her, along with birth control pills, as if she'd known which would be useful and which would be for show. He tore at her shirt like he was tearing up weeds. Tugged the pants over her bottom. She twisted and squirmed, and his nails dug into her hips. She choked on a veil of dust. Stones stabbed her shoulders. Thorns pierced her thighs.

The Lizard untangled himself slowly. Stood over her. A ragged giant blocking the moonlight. He nudged her face with a sand-caked boot. Nudged her breasts, nudged her belly. Said she was not too bad, but he'd had better. His tone amused. Like he was kidding, having a fun joke with her.

Then he searched the ground. She sat up, shirt in tatters, jeans wadded around an ankle. The warm glaze of The Lizard's sweat and saliva on her face, she wiped her breasts. Blood dripped like syrup from her mouth.

"Stand up," he said.

He held something the moon had brightened in his hand. She stood while trying to wrap herself in torn clothing. The panties were white with lavender flowers. He held them stretched out and displayed. A blunt finger wiggled through the ragged hole in the crotch. She looked away. He shoved the panties into her face. Headlights far off came toward them. She realized they were near the highway. He took her hand and turned it palm up. He tapped the upturned hand, dictating that she keep it up. She did as he wanted. He spread the panties over her palm.

"Hang them in the tree," he said.

She didn't understand, stood shaking and looking.

"The tree," he said.

He grabbed the back of her neck and forced her toward the tree. Then she saw it outlined in moonlight. Tears rolled down her face. She hung her panties over a thick branch. They drooped like a white flower. At that moment, the headlights swung by, and she saw five other pairs and a torn bra hanging on the branches beside hers.

•

She bolted upright. The rain had stopped, but the wind now moaned against the cottage. She sat a moment with the blanket trapped between her legs. She turned off the television, set out clothing for the night, and stepped into the shower. She washed her hair. The Lizard's face was a smudge in her memory. But not all of it. The narrow shape of his black eyes, unforgettable. She dressed and went to her car. The wind tore at her hair and made the door difficult to open. After buckling herself in, she sat still in the gently rocking car and stared at herself in the mirror. He did not remember her. She was one of many. One of countless, nameless, forgettable faces. But she did not forget him. Certain of the narrow shape, certain of the color, as black as unmined coal. She had no doubt. The Lizard was Flaco.

SevenEight

SevenEight left Reynolds's cruiser and headed for the beach. He rode the elevator to the fifteenth floor of a high-rise condo. A Dupuis thug let him inside with instructions to take off his shoes.

He unlaced his Timberlands and plunked them against the wall. Children scampered past, squealing and laughing. Dupuis's wife, a sweet slab of delicious, emerged from a bedroom. She was slim and younger than Dupuis. Beneath her robe, pretty little pokies designed to hobble a man pushed against the silk. He could hardly breathe, figured he'd need a claw hammer to pry his eyes off her. Gave her a sticky sugar sound, Mm, and said he'd come to see Dupuis.

She touched her hair, a silky move to match the fabric of her robe.

"On the balcony."

"Yes, ma'am," he said, but he was thinking about the cat flaps between her thighs.

He stepped over toys. Another thug relaxed on the couch with a morning paper. Smoking a cigarette next to him sat a man with horn-rimmed glasses. A cut-and-stitch man, he'd heard, whose enthusiasm for healing was outgunned only by his passion for prolonging another's suffering. Fingers long and thin, and he appeared to be in some sort of meditative trance.

SevenEight dodged two girls racing from one room to the next. A goddamn regular domestic scene. He caught sight of

Dupuis in billowing boxers on the balcony. Wind tossed the net curtains. A small table held glasses and napkins fluttered by gusts from the Gulf.

"It's so fucking hot." Dupuis held a gin tonic to his forehead. He indicated the table. "Have one."

He didn't want no pussyass drink but took it anyway. "Just what I needed." He made a lip-smacking *Ah* to emphasize his pleasure.

"How do you like this?" Dupuis pointed at the Gulf of Mexico like it was a bum sleeping on his doorstep. "Brought the wife and kids out for a little sun-and-fun. And look at this shit."

"Goddamn bitch all right."

"It's enough to wipe the tan off your face."

"You already know."

Dupuis turned from the balcony. His belly fell ugly over his crotch like he'd strapped a hog across it. He sat on a wide chair.

"What do you got for me?"

SevenEight set down the gin and tonic. "Shipment. Huge. Cartel out of Mexico. Got a man to insure it."

"Where?"

"En La Playa. Night after next."

"Not a chance." Dupuis balanced his drink on the plateau of his belly. "No reputation, no history, no references. No deal."

SevenEight laughed. "Dig this. Nigger got to get his spurs on somewhere. My time to ride."

Dupuis wasn't smiling. He seemed intent on staring down the storm.

"Check around, baby," SevenEight said. "I'm all good."

"This ain't pimping whores. And cut out that baby shit. I ain't your baby."

Dupuis wiped his shoulders with the dripping silvery glass. "It's so fucking hot. And this business is hot. Too hot for this ass-end of the universe town."

SevenEight smiled. "What I be thinking exactly."

He scooted the chair forward and oiled his mouth with a cube of ice.

"See, blud, sheriff and me's sharing a bone. Got me a nigger on the inside. And that's immunization. For you, for me. All of us. Damn, it's a fucking cure for cancer. Plus."

He let the hook hang. Could hardly contain himself, wanted to bust out laughing, wanted to shove the fat man over the railing and watch him explode on the cement below. Splatter like a sack of shit, and he'd laugh. He'd laugh snot hard. Could hardly stand it. He refocused on the heft of the man in the wide chair. The entirety of him had to be nothing but a thick, yellow jelly. He waited, letting the hook hang there, and then he got it back. A glance. An eyebrow of interest.

"Plus. Word is you prop up for a certain activity." He sat back and sipped the bitter liquid. Maybe the wife don't know what the fat man do, he thought, but it all over, the man's hatred for women—and the savage joy he get from destroying them. Or maybe she do, and wear Dupuis's brand, like all the others. The ones that can't fight back, that's how he picked them, addicts, immigrants, debtors—only to crush them hard beneath the heel of his boot. Word about: rope-bound women, leather cutting through skin, the choked purple surfaces and bright smears of blood. Beatings with fists and steel-toes, baseball bats. The fat smile of the man as he inflicts pain, and she's on her knees, dazed—but he'd never let her go lights out—no fun in that—and then the knives, shiny and sharp as a nick o' time, and he help himself to a trophy—an ear, a tongue, a clit, a foot, a finger—and she be begging to die, just begging, and what she don't know, he be all boned-up the more she cry for death, and he advance into the pleasure dome and top it off with the charcoal smell of branded flesh. And then the man in the horn-rimmed glasses, who be licking his chops the whole while, he certify with his patchwork that the woman, and the memory, will survive. And who know, SevenEight reflected, what one had the greater joy.

A bumpy flow of recognition rippled along Dupuis's fat face.

SevenEight smiled. "That's right. You hearin' me. I'm doing Office Max for your pleasure."

Dupuis's wife stepped barefoot onto the balcony.

Dupuis turned. He rested his hands on his belly and played with the silver ring on his finger.

She set down a tray of drinks and kissed the top of Dupuis's head.

"Dude named Blasko tells me there's paperless workers at En La Playa." SevenEight shook the ice around. "No surprise in that."

Dupuis's wife stood at the railing and looked over the water. The wind played a game of hide and peek with the silk and the waterslide backs of her thighs.

SevenEight sucked it deep and turned his attention back to Dupuis.

"Like I be saying. Amnaj, he in real deep doo doo. Will hand the shit over like that. Guaranteed."

Dupuis held up a finger. His belly rose like a whale from the ocean when he touched his wife's hand.

"Take it inside, honey."

The wind swirled and knocked over a yellow plastic sand bucket. Dupuis's wife scooped it up on her way out.

"Strange shambles," Dupuis said. His gaze turned toward the Gulf. "The Soviet Union fell, and we cheered. But Sorana's Moldovan." He looked inside after his wife. "After the collapse, the borders were like a sieve. New Orleans was going international, and I was a worker bee, maximizing profits. Ten percent of Moldova's women were sold into prostitution. She was the right age. Easy prey for the slave trafficker's snare. I saved her. There was a look in her eye. A virtuous look I couldn't ignore."

Dupuis's hand traveled with his breath from his chest to his belly.

"Very strange shambles," he said. "You save one, you kill another." His eyes seemed to vacation on a pensive thought. "You think I'm talking about respect, but I'm talking about honor. I saved her. Felt right. She deserved something better."

SevenEight swallowed an ice chip. "Yeah, that's a sad one all right. Real goddamn sad story."

"You have a fat mouth and no honor," Dupuis said. "And what I'm telling you is never speak of business in the presence of my wife. You're a smart man and a smart man like you, he wanna avoid a bullet fuck."

A thug set a bowl of sliced oranges on the table. SevenEight needed the intrusion and stared at the wet red meat snug in the rinds. He took one and released his anger into the bite, the juice dribbling like blood down his chin. All he could think. Fat motherfucker's gonna die. Gonna slap a hole between your eyes and watch you capsize on the pavement. He chewed the pulp, pushed the rind against his teeth, and sucked the fire from it.

The wind stalled. He looked at Dupuis. He seemed visionary, staring over the water as if something ruthless were clawing its way toward him. That's right, motherfucker. That's me coming after your fat ass.

Dupuis clasped his hands across his chest. His mood seemed to shift with the wind. He spoke with a light tone. "You following the Cooler Baby?"

"It's all you hear."

"I bet they find it. What do you think?"

"Who gives a shit?"

"What do you think?"

"Not a chance."

"No?"

"No."

SevenEight laughed his way to his car. He had Dupuis. He mashed the music button and pulled into traffic. He felt fuck-happy-good slumped deep in his ride. The hood rich with color. The load smooth over asphalt. He looked good, felt good. He had Dupuis. Had that fat motherfucker.

In the rearview he saw a red car. He shook his head. A piece of shit compared to his ride. He imagined dealing cars and pitching that red piece of shit: We got fugly cars, and we got fugginugly cars, but for a special price—he saw himself slapping the hood—for a special price, we got muddafug-ginugly cars. He couldn't stop laughing.

It was all working out. He was going to the top. Couldn't stop laughing. After Dupuis had done his thirty-mile zone on the Cooler Baby, he'd wanted to talk about the offer to satis-fy his sadistic tastes. He knew dead straight what he wanted. Bet he had a massive boner attack thinking about it. He didn't even have to ask. He knew already and said it like he was or-dering the seafood platter.

"I want the little Thai girl."

Joom Janpong

ON THE WAY TO THE superstore, they heard that the Cooler Baby had been found.

"I would die of happiness," Joom said.

Rain splattered against the windshield.

"My heart would leap from my chest," Nokyung said.

Feeder bands swirled in whites and grays across the sky. Joom fanned her fingers against the window. "Do you think it's incredible?"

Nokyung turned the wipers low. "Unbelievable. This morning they were going to give up the search. I saw that on television. They said they would stop looking, and I felt miserable."

"But now you see," Joom said as she listed items on a receipt book. "Everyone has hope."

The parking lot was full. Crowds gathering supplies. They pulled into a space near the back.

Joom got out. "Even the rain has stopped."

As she tied her hair into a ponytail, she sensed a shift in the atmosphere. She stood close to Nokyung. Nokyung gazed at the sky as if she, too, felt the difference.

A man climbed out of his truck. He was beaming and waving his arms. "You hear the news?" He was shouting. "They found the Cooler Baby. They found it."

The change had been swift. An hour ago, they had slogged heavy-hearted through the wind and the rain. They had come to the store to prepare for a terrible storm. The news of the Cooler Baby arrived like a good omen. People smiled, talked, moved with ease and gladness. Their strides were filled with hope that defied the slate-colored gloom above.

"Water first," Nokyung said, pushing the cart. "Then batteries, candles, matches, laxatives—"

"Laxatives?"

"That's what Uncle said."

"You think he meant stool softener?"

"He said laxatives."

"He should eat prunes."

"That's what I told him."

"Prunes and lots of water."

"And for some reason, he wants lighter fluid. And latex gloves."

"He's going to roast a pig," Joom said. "That's what he told me. He calls it a hurricane party."

"And look at this. An electric carving knife!"

"Right. Like we're no longer capable."

They strolled past an enraptured crowd watching the news on the wide screens.

"He's crazy," Nokyung said, "thinking he will have a pig roasting during this storm, and do you know who's going to be carving out in the rain?"

Joom made a face, us, and they laughed.

They wheeled through an aisle of dual-flush toilet converters and crystal cleaners. A man seemed to be following them.

"I want to go to the Asian store next," Nokyung said, "to get candles for the altar."

Joom resisted glancing back. "I arranged flowers this morning," she said.

Earlier, she stopped by their uncle's house to cut mint and lemon grass for the food they would prepare at the bar. She went inside. The house was spare. A floor futon. Some old bar stools around the kitchen counter. A portrait of the king, stately in his uniform, hung on the wall. Beds stacked with clothing. A teak cabinet that held photos of their relatives. In a hallway nook, several tables layered in height, a Buddha on the highest level, pictures of their dead grandparents on the next. Within this structure, candles, fresh flowers, and white string for blessings. She prepared a meal of rice and mango and fixed the plate on one of the tables. Then she straightened the rooms. When she finished, she said goodbye to her grandparents.

"Do you pay respects?" Joom lifted cases of bottled water.

"Yes, of course." Nokyung crouched. She stacked cases on the lower rack of the cart.

"So do I, but not as much as I used to."

"I miss Ma."

"I miss her, too, but it's not that." The man who'd been following loitered by cereal boxes. Joom turned away. "Lately, I forget to put the food out, or I go by without thinking about it."

"You are busy and tired. It is easy to be distracted."

Joom came around the cart and crouched near her sister.

"Do you remember the giant crab in Cha am?"

"What about it? Is this enough water?"

"A few more." She lifted a case. "The crab was always after me in dreams. It's that feeling again. We wanted to come here, right? This was a good idea?"

Nokyung pulled back her hair. She sat crouched with her forearms on her knees.

"We are here. Help with the water."

"I'm confused sometimes. The Americans want me to be American. Do you know what I mean? To be like them. Uncle says we have to 'fit in.' But what I know now is that this country will never protect me."

Nokyung loaded the last case of water. "What do you talk about?"

She pulled Nokyung up by the hand. "It is too big now, an exaggeration, like the giant crab, to think I can have a place here."

Nokyung sighed. "I want to go home, too, ตัวเอง. But we are here. Let's not try to be happy or unhappy. Let's just get what we need. And go."

They rolled into the meat section. Joom glanced back. The man had followed. She noticed him first while they were gathering batteries. He next appeared in the bottled water aisle. Now he peered into the meat display case. He wasn't shopping, though he turned packages, as if looking for a particular cut of meat.

She nudged Nokyung. "Over there."

She glanced. "That man."

Nokyung lifted her eyes and sighed.

"You know him?

She nodded.

The man seemed to realize he'd been spotted and steered his cart toward them.

"Don't look," Joom said. "He's coming."

Nokyung swung the cart. "Let's go."

They were cornered against the meat case and the man's cart.

"Hello," the man said. He indicated the cases of water. "After last minute supplies?"

The greeting had been meant for Nokyung. A blush spread across her face. But she also lowered her head, her eyes. When she lifted her head, she gave him the bar smile. The one that said she smiled only because she had to.

Nokyung said, "Nice ring," with a slight gesture, a smirky lip.

The man slid his hand out of sight. A chagrined smile stretched out. "The thing we can't get past."

"You were at the bar last night," Joom said. "There with Ray Reynolds. You were there, and then you left."

"Yes. Derek Stickleback." He extended his hand and lowered it when she didn't accept it. "I recognize you from the bar, as well. You are?"

"Joom Janpong. Nokyung's sister."

He seemed to stare at them, first her, then Nokyung. "I should have guessed. The nieces of?"

"Amnaj Boonngamanong," Joom said.

He laughed. "Well, I won't try to pronounce that. He's the owner of En La Playa?"

Joom nodded. She glanced at Nokyung. What was she doing? This Stickleback clearly had an eye for her, and she was checking out the price per pound of tenderloin. She saw how he longed to remain with them but also how his body shifted with discomfort. He was her chance, and she was ignoring him.

"Well," he said, after a bit, "I guess I'll get going. Nice to see you again."

Nokyung flashed the bar smile.

Stickleback disappeared behind an aisle of fish seasonings.

"That was stupid," Joom said. "He likes you."

"You saw the ring."

"He likes you. Don't you see that? It's your chance."

They pushed toward paper products.

Nokyung sighed. "I don't have a feel for him. I don't like farang."

"A feel? He likes you. What do you need a feel for?"

"You don't care who you sleep with, do you? Married or not? But I do. Don't make me out bad."

"You have to take a chance." They walked apart from each other, the cart in the middle. "You never know who's married. That's what Uncle says."

"What does he know? Wasn't he married? Didn't he lose his wife? I don't want that. Will you let me be what I want?"

They tossed paper towels into the cart.

"It's worth a chance, isn't it? That's what Uncle says. Maybe he's separated, maybe divorced. I know! His wife died. It could be. She died, and he doesn't know what to do with the ring."

Nokyung transferred a package of toilet paper into the cart. "You make too much of things. Let's go."

Nokyung sped away. Joom trotted after. She was about to say something when a collective groan flooded the superstore. People ran to the televisions. What happened? Is it true?

Joom and Nokyung wended through the appliance section toward the slack assembly frozen in front of twenty televisions. Their faces reflected the dull colors of light from the massive waves and swirling toss of clouds onscreen. A voice came loud and sudden. A correction of an earlier broadcast. The announcer spoke in a grim, flat tone. "The Cooler Baby remains lost at sea."

Amnaj Boonngamanong

THE GLOOM OF AFTERNOON dissolved into the gloom of evening with little difference. He stood behind the counter and observed his nieces arranging clear shrimp soup and spicy ground beef on the serving table. He'd come in through a squall, but the airy sound of Thai music from the karaoke machine had already erased the miserable screech of the storm.

A flat-panel screen showed a woman walking among rain trees and singing to the sky about a man she had loved and lost. Nokyung and Joom began to dance to the music. Their arms gracefully angled. Their hands delicate and extended like the beaks of cranes.

Castro stopped writing and turned with the glass of iced Corona in hand to be enthralled by the tranquil movement of the girls. "Where are they?"

"The bank of the Kok River." He wiped the counter with a cloth. "Blue morning mountains in the distance."

Castro leaned on an elbow. "An aqueous motion. It's surreal."

"It's called the Curtain Dance." He wiped the inside of a glass. "In ancient times, a northern city was divided, and a knight from one side was made prisoner by the other side, and both sides were threatened by an invading Chinese army. The captured knight agreed to fight a Chinese knight and defeated him, and the Chinese retreated. This knight was given half the city and the daughter of the king. The knight accepted, but only if the god of the city would not call him slave. Thai will not be slave. And so, this is the veiled dance, the Curtain Dance of the wedding."

He touched Castro's journal. "Write that."

"Write it?"

"Thai is only Asian country never to be colonized. Write it."

"I will write it."

Castro opened the book and wrote in large letters. The pen cut deep into the page. The words were bold and broad. Strong, straight lines beneath the words.

"Read it," he said, taking up another glass.

"You want me to read it?"

He nodded and wiped the inside of a glass.

"Thai will not be slave. Thai is free."

He fixed a keen gaze on Castro.

"Now, you understand."

He felt a soft hip and turned. Katia squeezed between him and the cooler to fix trays of cherries, lemons, and limes.

"They dream of home," she said.

He glanced at Castro. "You see? She knows."

Instead of moving aside, he remained still and let her body massage his. Admired the deft way her hands arranged the fruits. He laughed gently.

"Someday, I will take you to visit," he said to her. "I know a cafe on the Chao Phraya River. A beautiful sunset and a bowl of noodles."

"Your yearly offering," she said without looking. "Always someday."

Katia stocked the call shelf. He found himself watching her

hips rise and fall, the blouse climb her back, a luster of sweat on her spine. He shook his head, turned back, and laughed.

Castro was smiling. "Hard to hide it." He sipped the Corona.

Amnaj scoffed. "A rabbit dreams of the moon."

Castro shook the ice. "Whatever you say." He held the cup still. "Do you know the poetry of Neruda? No? Chilean. If not the best ever, firmly fixed on the short list. He writes somewhere about the body of a woman."

"Who doesn't?"

Castro sipped. "'To survive myself I forged you like a weapon,' he writes. 'Like an arrow in my bow, a stone in my sling. But the hour of vengeance falls, and I love you. Body of skin, of moss, of eager, and firm milk.'"

He thought a moment, flipped a napkin idly. "I guess that's OK."

Katia inserted herself between them. "You're wasting your time, Castro. He don't know poetry unless it comes out of the tap." She swatted Amnaj with a damp rag.

He brushed her off. "We're doing the talking. Go find work to do." He turned back to Castro. "Thai have a famous poet."

Castro opened the book. "Tell me about it."

He drew up, hands flat on the counter.

"The king of Ayutthaya had a favorite poet. His name was Sri. There were no last names in those days. People called him Sri Pracht, and this means guru or philosopher. He had an affair with one of the governor's wives, and the governor found out and ordered him to be killed. Sri wrote his last poem on the ground with his big toe at the place where was executed:

ธรณีนี่นี้　　　　เป็นพยาน
เราก็ศิษย์มีอาจารย์　หนึ่งบ้าง
เราผิดท่านประหาร　เราชอบ
เราบ่ผิดท่านมล้าง ดาบนี้ คืนสนอง

"The tone," Castro said. "I expected defiance, but there's sadness or disappointment." He readied his pen. "Tell me in English."

"Threshold of earth. Witness. You have a wise teacher but I also have a wise teacher. If I'm wrong, and you kill me, then I accept it. If I am not wrong, this sword has the night.—It is a warning to the governor. If the governor is wrong, the sword will go back to him. Later, the king learned that his favorite poet had been executed without permission. The sword then had the night. And the king ordered the execution of the governor."

Castro set the pen down. "Sri reproves the governor, but I hear the disappointment, and I don't know why."

He crossed his arms. "Disappointment, yes. Maybe he reprove the governor, or all of us, that we have not learned anything about love."

Castro tapped. "In the land of Buddha, the sword and execution—tell me, Amnaj, honestly, what is the character of the Thai people?"

He poured the remainder of Castro's Corona.

"Once I saw a woman in the market. She was buying something unimportant, a table mat. She gave the seller one hundred baht—about three dollars. The seller pinched the bill but did not accept it and said, 'One fifty.' The woman held the bill tight. 'One hundred,' she said. Both squeezed the ends of the bill. One-fifty, the seller said. One-hundred. The bill like a rope pulled between them. 'One fifty.' 'One hundred.' A pause the length of a breath. And the seller relented."

Castro prepared to write. "And this is the Thai character?"

"No." He leaned on his elbows. "Above it all, the whole time, they were both smiling."

The door flew open. A sweltering wind rushed inside. The storm had entered En La Playa once more. He called to Blasko. "Shut the door."

Blasko came inside but didn't shut the door. He stood swaying with rain splashing behind. Leaving Castro, he went around the counter past Nails, who was working out bank shots and waiting for the Mexicans. He could tell Blasko had started early today and figured he'd come in to sleep it off. He led Blasko by the arm to a corner chair. "What a mess you are." Blasko appeared ready to cry. "What a mess."

SevenEight stood in the doorway. He glanced at Blasko. "Thought I took a wrong turn and wound up at the fucking homeless shelter."

"Shut the door."

SevenEight bullied up. "It's coming, Amnaj. Big storm coming." He opened up a gold grin. "Best hold on to your ass tight." He looked around and laughed. "Yes, sir. Big-ass storm. You ain't gonna know it till you're flopping on the floor like a goddamn fish."

Reynolds pushed through the door. Behind him filed the Mexicans, all shaking off rain.

"What are you saying?"

"I'm just saying."

SevenEight flexed his hands and sauntered to the bar. He pointed at Maria who was tapping out beer for Reynolds. "Chiquita, mm-mm. Got you some sweet stuff going on tonight. Get me one, too, and a shot of Jack. We gon' party party tonight, baby."

He left Blasko in the corner, kept an eye on SevenEight. Something was up.

SevenEight grabbed a chair next to Reynolds and threw down the shot. He bounced up and turned to Nokyung and Joom. "Turn that fucking shit off. This ain't no goddamn China. Goddamn fucking screech music give a nigger a headache. Need us some groove nasty, baby. Get that on."

SevenEight was always outlandish, but this was something else. He could feel it in the length of his thighs, the expansion of his ribs.

He strode to the bar, wary. Nokyung called out in Thai, "What do you want us to do?" The door opened. Warm, wet wind at his back. He turned. Dupuis shook himself inside. He was with a thug. And closed an umbrella.

He intended to have a word with SevenEight. But now pulled a deep breath and reminded himself to keep a cool heart. He'd see how things developed. He looked at Nokyung. "Change it."

Then, behind the counter, he called Maria and noticed a strange thing. SevenEight had Reynolds by the chin. He had the chin clasped between a thumb and two fingers. Moved Reynolds's head up and down, as if checking to see if the neck still worked. And grinning. He was grinning at Reynolds, who sat there and let it happen.

He saw at the end of the bar that Castro was also intrigued by this pantomime. Their eyes met. Castro shrugged and returned to writing.

"Yes, sir?" Maria stood close. Beyond her, Katia, watching.

He waited until Dupuis found a table. Picked the corner where Blasko was in a sprawled stupor. The thug poked Blasko. Blasko's head latched to the wall. The thug scraped an old cigarette butt from an ashtray and stuck it in Blasko's mouth. He dumped the ashes on the sagged head and laughed.

He told Maria to serve the Mexicans.

She blanched.

"You OK?"

She stammered. "Nothing, I just." She indicated Dupuis. "You wanted me to wait on him. For Joom."

"I'll take care of it. Serve the Mexicans."

The night was strange. Had a different feel. Something happening, and he didn't know what. Quick survey of the bar. Others had arrived. Blasts of wind at their backs. Maybe that was it. The way the air circulated the coming storm. Nokyung and Joom spread out, took orders, opened tabs. Promote the hurricane party, he'd told them. Nokyung looked at him. She wasn't going to do it. Up to you, her look said. But Joom went about gaily. She'd tell everyone what fun they'd have. They'd come just to be with her. He'd have to nag Nokyung. Then, out of duty, she'd also tell them. But she'd say it like she was spreading a disease. Such a plain, hopeless girl. And Maria, usually enthusiastic. She'd been serving the Mexicans for months, so what was different tonight? A snap of temper in her eyes when he'd told her to serve them. That wasn't like her. What was it? Had her eye on Joel. He'd embarrassed her. The way she blushed, it was obvious. And the darker one, Flaco, he was harmless. So, what was it? The wind. Maybe. A dark, tropical taste that lingered long after the rain had evaporated.

He stirred when SevenEight rose from the counter and left Reynolds with a light slap to the cheek. Cocked his way over to Dupuis and eased into a chair. A strange intensity discharging from the fat man. Something not right. His bones tingled with an odd sensation. A pervasive sense of danger. They were talking and laughing, but it was different. They looked at him, they looked at the girls, and they were talking and laughing. The thug grinning, also laughing.

Feeling his face cumbered with dread, he decided to find out.

"Didn't I say it?" SevenEight kicked out a chair. "Here's our man." He looked at Dupuis. "Said it, didn't I? Nigger knows what's going on."

Dupuis motioned. "Please, join us."

He felt heavy and sick. "I'll stand."

Dupuis gestured. "Please. Do us the honor."

Blood iced through his body. Bones tingled. "I'm fine. I'll stand."

Dupuis brought his hands together on his fat chest. He sighed. "Here I am, and you dishonor me. I bring money to your establishment, and you disrespect me. Come now. Sit."

"I don't want your money."

Dupuis shook his head. The jowls blobbed across the face. He spoke to SevenEight. "I'm afraid you are wrong.

My friends at immigration will not like this place at all." He turned. "Sit."

Amnaj snatched the chair up. Blood stinging his veins, beating through his head. Cocked the chair. An angle of attack.

A hand clasped his shoulder.

"Set it down." A soft voice. Reynolds. Sad, beaten down. "I don't want to arrest you." The face a gray basin of pain. "Set it down and sit. Please."

He sat.

SevenEight squirmed. "Motherfucker never made a better decision in your life. Nigger, you just don't know, just don't know who you be fucking with."

He stared at Dupuis. Smug savagery stitched into the matter-of-fact shit grin. A single diamond earring announcing its own cred. Eyes the color of copper and, the longer he stared, he noted as if in contradiction a strange contrast, a hint of prescience or fear or sadness in the sunken part of the eyes, and possibly because of the way the light was hitting the skin, the dull waxing texture of dead flesh. He wanted to see it clearly, to understand it, but SevenEight, gesturing and wiggling like he had to piss, broke it up.

"Got no clue who you be fucking with. Just don't know. You in deep, man. Shit deep. Need to be hearing this, nigger. Time in Miami some badass motherfucker name of fucked up Jack Samsom go in the tank in round eight. Pretty little Olympic dive. Thing you know next?" SevenEight chopped his wrist and laughed. "No more badass motherfucker."

Dupuis glanced at the thug. The thug grabbed SevenEight's arm and shook him.

"He got a big mouth. Forget him," Dupuis said. His chin bobbed like debris on a grim ocean. His eyes narrowed. "Let's deal."

Nokyung Janpong

"Some storm," she said, and uncapped a Corona and poured it into a cup of ice. "It's coming right at us. Ever see one like it?"

Castro squeezed lime, swirled the cup, brought it to his lips. "You know how to make them."

She laughed. "What did I do?"

"It's a rough storm, but there's been worse. And worse to come. Sometimes you just have to hold on until it passes." He sipped again, licked his lips. "All you can do. Hold on. And clean up afterward. That's the important part. Do that right, and all's well."

"Means?" She was looking at Amnaj and Maria. Maria seemed shaken up. He was probably getting on to her for coming in late.

"I'm not surprised," Castro said.

"So sad about the Cooler Baby."

"Haven't heard that today."

"Do you care?"

"It's not that." He swirled the ice. "I'm practical."

Amnaj stood alone, gazing, lingering at Dupuis's table.

"How do you mean that?"

"The Cooler Baby will survive. Or not." He closed the notebook, "But I won't have anything to do with it. I'll tell you, though." He put the pen in his pocket. "If it survives, then it will be special."

"You believe it?"

"Indeed." He crossed his arms over the bar, over the note-book. "We'll be talking about it for decades."

"That's a long time."

"Because it's special."

Amnaj moved toward Dupuis, and the reach of his bantam stride told her he was angry. She felt pulled to go to him, stand with him.

"They called off the search," Castro said.

"What?"

"They called it off."

"But the Cooler Baby—"

"Too dangerous. That storm's a cat four."

"How will it survive?"

Castro shrugged. "It won't. But in 1971, Juliane Koepcke was in flight over the Peruvian rainforest. She was seventeen years old, traveling with her mother. Lightning struck the plane. Still strapped to her seat, she fell two miles into the jungle. The fall broke her collar bone. She followed the downhill path of a river for nine days until she found a lean-to. The lumberjacks who chanced upon her paddled seven hours to civilization. Everyone else on board died. But she survived."

She went around the counter. What was Amnaj doing? He'd lifted a chair, looked ready to throw it at Dupuis. Then Reynolds had come up. Amnaj then sat at the table. The grim way he sat, tension in his hands.

She looked at Castro. He'd seen it, but he appeared unfazed. He continued speaking. "And in 1942, twenty-four-year-old Poon Lim sailed on the Ben Lomond as a steward.

In the south Atlantic, the ship was torpedoed by a German U-boat. He jumped into the ocean with a lifejacket—the poor fellow was no swimmer—and the ship sank in three minutes. He survived for one hundred and thirty-three days. Brazilian fishermen eventually found him. Ninety-seven men died— the entire crew. But Poon Lim survived."

She felt sick. Amnaj called Joom. Joom was walking toward the table.

"Survival, in the strictest sense," Castro said, "is about brute force."

"I must go." She flew past him, past the counter, past Katia, trying to stop her. She clasped Joom, stood next to her as a shield.

Amnaj spoke to Joom. "Go with them. Go now."

She locked Joom's arm. "What's this all about?"

"Back to work," Amnaj said.

She tugged. But Joom held fast, hesitating or confused.

"Do as I say."

He looked rough and damaged. His tone gruff yet restrained. "Leave her."

She could not refuse her uncle, and she would not leave her sister, so she stood between them, body burning, and in her hands, Joom had become limp. Dupuis removed a banded stack of bills from a pocket and dropped it on the table in front of Amnaj.

She clutched Joom. "I can't believe—why do you do this?"

Amnaj rubbed a hand across his face. A resigned sigh, and his eyes were on the money. He looked at Dupuis. "Now you shame me. This could have waited."

She shook the table. "Not her. Me. I'll go with you."

Dupuis, hand to mouth, the ring sparkling against his lips, looked at her as if not looking at her, as if denying her presence. His corpulent lips swelled into a dismissive smile.

"I don't want you."

Then he addressed Amnaj. "Seems you have no respect anywhere. Not even in your own house."

Amnaj slammed the table. He grabbed her by the throat and drove her to the counter. She beat on his shoulders and scratched at his face. He shouted at Katia to come. Katia pinned her arms.

She felt separated from herself. Through a fog, she heard Katia tell Amnaj, "This isn't right. You know it. You know it isn't."

She began to cry. Amnaj turned away. Turned slowly and then stopped. The narrow and hateful eyes of Jimmy Nails.

Amnaj glared. "What are you staring at?"

Jimmy Nails pursed his lips, shrugged his shoulders. "Nothing, man." He turned back to the game. "Nothing at all."

She struggled against Katia's grip. Quick Spanish whispers she didn't understand filled her ears and became murmurs across the surface of her shaking body.

Over Katia's shoulder, she saw Dupuis and Joom leave. It had happened fast. They were there, then they were gone. The wind howled inside. Rain splashed onto the floor. SevenEight appeared behind Katia. He grinned, laughed. Over Katia's shoulder, she struck at him. He jumped back.

Then SevenEight said something to Katia. She felt Katia's body tremble, the rainy smell of her breath. She imagined

SevenEight had given her a job. That's how Katia reacted, in horror and submission. The tremors of acquiescence.

She couldn't tell who needed support now. She moved slowly, shaking off Katia's grip. Beyond Katia, Amnaj sat at the table where Dupuis had been. Alone, and with his elbows resting on his knees, face in his hands.

She looked at Katia. "Why?" She couldn't say any more. Sobs choked her voice.

"Calmate, calmate," Katia said. "You don't know these men, niña. They would have killed him."

Katia Molino

From the end of the bar, she saw the whole thing. Saw what everyone else saw, and more. Dupuis, plump at the table and next to him his thug. And then SevenEight joined them. Amnaj came in haste and determination. But he was shaking. Something she'd never seen before. Fear pounded in his chest, crippled each step toward the table. And then Joom, cowering like a beaten dog. They talked awhile. Amnaj submissive and trembling. Joom cowering and limp. Then Nokyung flying past. The rage ripening on her face, swelling in her fists. Amnaj, torn in two. His countenance a patchwork of fright and impotence. Dupuis gloated, his bulbous face rose and fell like the massive swells of the Gulf, his laughter saturated with the domination of these poor people. She saw what everyone saw. But also what they didn't see. Behind Dupuis, Blasko tongued the cigarette from his mouth. He was not dead to the world, as they'd imagined. He was alert. He was patient. The cigarette fell into his lap. No one else noticed. The cigarette fell into his lap, and he left it there.

She clung to Nokyung. The girl was furious, unrelenting, and she hung on. Wrapped her up and held on. Furious with Amnaj that he would sell his niece. Enraged that he had submitted without a fight. But also the pain in his eyes. The indecision. The terror. Nokyung cried and struggled, and she held on tight and whispered into the small girl's ear and glared at Amnaj. She couldn't stand the defeat reddening his eyes, the way he appeared bound and helpless. She hadn't stayed at En La Playa all these years for this. He turned away and swayed and buckled. She whispered into Nokyung's ear. Stroked her face and held on but felt within her breast that it was Amnaj who needed her. And she longed to hold him. Wished that she could take him in her arms and convince him that they would somehow get through. Then Jimmy Nails gave Amnaj a withering look, and she instantly hated him. As much as anyone, he should stand with Amnaj instead of looking down with disdain. She clung to Nokyung. Her body shook. It whimpered. Slowly, Nokyung descended into a maddening but calm resignation. She caressed Nokyung's face, whispered in her ear, felt her going limp against her breast. Amnaj at the empty table. His eyes shifted into a strange stare, as if the table held all the world, and he'd seen at once just how small and terrible it was.

"A man's coming."

SevenEight stood at her shoulder.

"What?"

"A man. Wears a fucking cowboy hat."

SevenEight, a rippling grin of cruelty on his face.

"Moment he come in, you already know it. Big fucking man. Tall. Tall fucking cowboy hat. Do him quick. Get the money first."

He was laughing. She saw that it was Amnaj, that it was Nokyung, the whole family that had kicked up his elation. And something more. Pride, she saw it, in the shine of his eyes, the tone of his voice. He couldn't see she was busy caring for Nokyung. As if she weren't there. He extended his arms, stretched them in a majestic pose. Puffed up pride. Something more, what? His peacocking made her sick. Whatever had happened, the result was that they'd all been downgraded to pawns for his pleasure. He thumped his chest. "You are looking at the goddamn kingpin of Midsummer." Shouting, laughing.

She felt a light touch on her shoulder and turned around and flattened a hand against her breasts. "Ay carajo, my asustaste. Don't come up on me like that."

"Why?"

"What's wrong with you, Maria?"

She thought Maria, too, had been frightened. But that wasn't it. Her eyes were sharp, cool, hard. She shuddered, recalling her father's tales of La Llorona, the weeping woman who drowned her children to be with the man she loved, who could not enter the afterlife and was forced to wander the earth in search of her children. She turned away, no longer able to stand Maria's deathly gaze.

SevenEight appeared as a shadow going past and stood next to Reynolds at the counter. Clasped Reynolds's chin in his palm. They were speaking. She couldn't hear what. The scorn in his face. Reynolds nodded. She felt suddenly cold. Maria had grasped her shoulder. The touch sent ice down her spine.

SevenEight then kissed Reynolds. The kiss lingered. Reynolds seemed to be falling. The way the hands splayed. The head went back. SevenEight pressed down roughly. Reynolds lost his shoulders. There was nothing to him. Nothing. Her husband had disappeared in the kiss. Awkward at first, the kiss developed its own strange, rugged passion. She felt something torn from her breast.

She looked away. Blasko stood unbalanced against the wall. The fight in his legs made him appear filled with purpose. He clung to the paneling and staggered past Amnaj, past the table and the small and terrible world that absorbed him.

She loosened the grip on Nokyung. The girl rested against her chest. Maria tugged her shirt.

"Why?" Maria said again. "¿Por qué es tan cruel?"

She held her tongue, resisted the chill of Maria's presence.

"Especially to that man," Maria said, "who does nothing to him? Why does he do it?"

She turned to snap at Maria, but her eye caught the stare of Jimmy Nails. Aloof and callous, he chalked the cue. His eyes seemed to burn. The bar had become silent except for the sleepy drift of house music. Their eyes met. Nails shook his head, shook off the emotion, and turned back to the pool table.

A noise. SevenEight scraped a chair. As he pushed off, he ran into Blasko. He grabbed the drunk and shook him. Blasko fell back onto a table but kept his balance. SevenEight sauntered past Amnaj to the door and disappeared into the storm.

"Why?" Maria said.

Maria's fingers bit into her shoulder. She twisted from the frosty grip.

She watched Reynolds. Waited, sensing that he would know and would look. They connected, and her heart sank. He needed her, but what could she do? He'd shoved her away. Running colors of shame and regret smeared his eyes. They cried for help. She unfastened Nokyung from her breast and prepared to race to his side. Then she hesitated. He'd already given up. The way his head swayed. He'd seen the end and had surrendered. She felt her lips moving. They formed desperate words. Hold on. She felt the intense mouthing. Hold on, hold on, I'm coming. But the voice died behind the teeth. Expressions as soundless as salty wind. She wanted to go to him. But she saw that it no longer mattered. As if crushed by the knowledge of his shame, his head had dropped listlessly onto his chest. She eased Nokyung onto a stool. Undid Maria's hands from her shirt, noticed how the girl's face seemed to have collapsed.

"It breaks my heart," Maria said. "Why? Why?"

She had no time. "Mind your own business."

She snapped harsher than she'd intended, but she had to get to him. She squared Reynolds and held him close. His breath spread warmly over her neck. He began to whimper. She clutched him fast to the body, so the sound could not escape. Over his shoulder, she saw Nokyung leaning on the counter, head in hands. Maria mindlessly wiped the counter. Reynolds in her arms and her eyes on the girls. The kiss played out again. SevenEight had taken her man. Why it did not infuriate her, she didn't know. Because it was all happening so fast. That's why.

She held him, stroked his face, murmured into his ear. He was her husband. But the feelings were shifting about like loose items in a boat. Less than love, a nurturing acceptance welled in her breast. He'd spurned her when he'd come home. Now that she could be there for him, could hold him, her feeling was nothing more than decency. He needed her, and she held him. Not because she loved him. This loss of feeling surprised her and then annoyed her. She held him because it was decent. SevenEight had done this. She had burned with hatred for months. Now this feeling gave way to acceptance. Simple enough to hold Reynolds. Simple and decent.

Amnaj still stared at the table. There was a man who deserved comfort, and there was no one for him. Nokyung was too upset. Maria went about distracted, dazed, and for what reason? And she didn't dare leave Reynolds alone.

Then Blasko staggered into view. He seemed to have a destination, a purpose, but was blind on his feet.

She turned away. Maria distractedly wiped the counter. Maria was a lucky girl. Ignorant of her fate. Maria couldn't imagine what SevenEight had in mind for her. Could have been Maria instead of Joom tonight. SevenEight had told her to groom Maria. She'd delayed as much as possible. But the time would come. Soon enough, he would do as he'd done to her. Take her into a room and destroy her. With bitterness, she recalled how SevenEight had come into their lives. How he'd taken control. Reynolds begged her to save them. "Just once," he'd said. "One time, and it's all over. Debts are paid, and we're free." He made a promise. She believed him because she loved him and had submitted herself to SevenEight for him. But it wasn't just one time. It was many times. Then with others. Then it was just what she did. Somewhere in all that confusion, she'd lost the self-respect and the will to walk away. Her mind drifted. Then became focused with curiosity.

Blasko found his way to Jimmy Nails. He grabbed one of Nails's hooks. Nails jerked free and motioned, Get out of the way. Blasko said something. Nails shook his head. Blasko nodded.

Then Nails's cue fell with a clatter. Even the music seemed to dissipate into a foggy anchored silence. Blasko pointed at the table where Amnaj was sitting. A sound poured from Nails. A bark. Then a howl of rage.

Maria dropped a glass. It shattered on the floor. Katia watched her clean up the pieces. Then an idea took hold. She held Reynolds away from her and looked at his brooding face. He needed to be nineteen again. When he was at his best. Optimistic, charged with hope. She was about to tell him the idea when she saw Nails pass money into Blasko's hand. He'd never do that. Not Jimmy Nails. Nails grabbed Blasko's arms. Blasko nodded his head, Yes. His whole wasted body shook. Yes, yes.

Blasko then chopped down hard on the wrist.

Nokyung Janpong

THE BAR MADE HER feel sick, so she went to her uncle's house to sleep. Fitful dreams and crying spells kept her awake. Her body felt torn and bruised. And Joom did not answer the phone.

Before dawn, she drove through the steady rain and gusts of wind to Bangkok Cleaners. She made tea and sat with Jit in front of the television. Fear heightened her concentration. Any minute she expected to hear a report about Joom.

The news broadcast advisories and the efforts of emergency crews to prepare the coast for the hurricane. The Cooler Baby was briefly mentioned, almost like an assurance, a statement intended to quell rumors. The search had been called off but would resume after the storm, making it seem it was still possible to find it. Evacuation orders for the island were issued.

"The bar will close," Jit said.

"Uncle says he will not close."

"He will have to."

"He is stubborn."

"He is stupid."

Was he? It wasn't clear in her mind. The blur of the previous night had made her think—or hope—that she had been dreaming. But Dupuis had taken Joom. Her uncle sat there and had done nothing. He had taken money, and Dupuis had taken Joom. And Katia told her they would have killed Amnaj. There was no one to turn to, and she felt sick.

"Are you all right?"

She considered telling Jit what had happened and struggled to keep her tongue still. The way Jit watched her, eyes inviting, urging her to say something. It would be around soon enough. Gossip meat to chew on. Jit would tell Jiiab, who'd tell Muu, who'd tell Maew, who'd tell Pook. The chatty contagion would spread throughout the community. But she wasn't going to start it.

The warm tea cleansed her mouth. "I am all right."

Jit touched her arm. "Are you sure?"

The cup clacked on the table. "Yes. I want to work."

Jit removed the cups.

She phoned again. The ringing abrupt like a heartbeat until it stopped. She whispered, Answer, answer, but could not coax a reply.

Then she became absorbed in pressing pants. Bathed her face in the steam. The work was hard, the focus intense. Soon, the detachment came easy, a flood of daydreams of the rice fields near Mae Ai. The long stretches of brilliant green. A lonely buffalo plodding along in the distance. She missed home.

She imagined her mother's close-cropped hair and dark brown skin. Her guarded, dayworn eyes, as she cooked outside on a butane stove beneath an awning in an alcove that led to the kitchen. Her large brown feet, like dusty rabbits, peeked from beneath a sarong. The orange-cream pattern of the sarong made her skin as golden as the rice fields in winter.

Nokyung smiled as one memory begat another.

Their mother sent her and Joom across the fields at night to take food in stacked silver trays to their grandmother.

During the crossing, they conjured grim, toothy ghosts that terrified them. More likely, the sounds they heard were wild dogs that had smelled the food. But how fast they had run, squealing, under the tender, black night.

She pressed the pants and wiped moisture from her face and seemed to inhale a distant, sweet fragrance.

The smell of jasmine rice, steam from the cooker, when the morning sunlight made the world glisten. From the house gate, she watched the barefoot monks softly advancing along the misty road. Rising out of their orange robes, their shaven heads appeared serene and apart from anything else she had ever known. Her mother carried rice and red curry in plastic bags to make merit. She removed her shoes, knelt, and laid the food in the black metal bowls that the monks held at their waists. The monks then placed copper lids over the black bowls. Her mother pressed her hands together and bowed. The monks chanted, and an intimate vibration penetrated the surface of things. The deep, enveloping song seemed not to come from the monks but from the depths of the ground.

She stopped pressing pants and stared at the upper press plate and then at the red emergency stop button. A sensation rippled through her body, taking hold of it, shaking it. She longed to go home. Tears began to blur the machine.

A wind drove into the back room, interrupting her sadness. It had come from outside and had swept away the steam and cooled her skin. She became aware then that someone had opened the door of the shop.

Jit stuck her head through the industrial strip curtain that divided the front from the back.

"That lieutenant man is here," she said with a nod that she should go out.

"What time is it?"

"Almost noon."

"Has it been that long?"

Jit frowned. "Come, come. What do you care what time it is? That man is here."

They passed each other through the PVC strips. Stickleback dripped with rain. He held out a ticket. She noticed he'd removed his ring, but the tan line told her all she needed to know.

She grabbed the ticket and found several shirts, neat on hangers in thin plastic.

"You have too many shirts," she said, "or you are very dirty."

She didn't smile, but he laughed.

He nodded toward the back. "The old woman said you have lunch now."

"She is confused. I don't eat lunch."

"A break then." He spread his hands next to the shirts on the counter. "Coffee or soft drink?"

She shook her head. His face became serious.

"Are you all right?" he said. "You seem distracted. Like something heavy on your mind."

"Heavy? What does it mean?"

He chuckled. "Heavy. You know. Like something bothers or upsets you."

"No. Nothing is heavy on me."

The wind rattled the windows. "Maybe you don't want to go out in that." He smiled. "I can bring coffee here."

"I don't drink coffee."

He shrugged. "Soft drink then."

"I like to work. I don't have time for break."

He turned to go, and she felt relieved. Then he turned back.

"So," he said. "I'm standing here dripping wet." He pointed at his chin. "And look, I have on my sincere face. Do you see it?" He seemed to follow her gaze, which had settled, she realized, on the ring finger.

"About that," he said, his tone still light. "Is that what you want to know? Are you asking me about that?"

She didn't want to hear lies and shook her head.

He smiled. "Really," he said, again pointing at his chin. "This is a sincere face."

"It does not matter."

"You are not to be convinced, are you?"

"I am leaving soon. So, it is not important."

"Leaving? Where?"

"I go home."

The rain slashed against the window.

"And I can't convince you. I mean, to have coffee."

"You can not."

He pursed his lips and stared at his hands. Something fluttered across his face. She guessed it was regret. That he'd seen in the tan line of his finger a long history of choices that at the time they were made must have seemed reasonable and good. Now, in the midst of the storm, in the middle of the laundry, where the counter separated them—as high and as formidable as a stone wall—he must have realized that whatever hope he'd had of making something new, she had crushed. She felt sad watching him work through this realization. Sad for him and then for herself because of what her uncle had said.

She was too selfish for anyone.

He rubbed his forehead and shuffled his feet. He found a pen and wrote something down.

"My card." He pushed it across the counter. "Cell number's on the back."

He glanced at the rain beating against the window.

"It's going to be rough. So, in case you want anything."

He smiled.

"In case you want coffee."

He opened the door. A blast of wind threw the card off the counter. She waited until he was gone and then stared at the card. Then crouched down and took it up between her fingers and read it. The words ran together. She wiped her eyes and stuck the card in her back pocket.

Jit carried plates of rice and green curry. "Why do you do that?"

She turned away; the food made her ill. She called Joom. No answer.

"Eat," Jit said.

They stood at the counter with forks and spoons. She ate with distraction. Then noticed Jit staring.

"What do you run from?"

She sighed. Jit was determined to find out. "Maybe I am the kind who can not love."

"You are afraid. Jing jing, it's true. What about? Tell me."

"I can not." She guided rice and eggplant onto the spoon but felt no strength to lift it. "Maybe." She released the utensils and held the counter. "Maybe if he will tell me he is not married."

"And you will trust it?"

"If he will tell me."

"You are the sort to put fear behind you? You can trust someone?"

"I don't know. Maybe."

Jit scraped rice and a piece of chicken onto her spoon. "Maybe," she repeated, her tone mocking. "Maybe. Maybe—maybe he is the kind of man who will not tell you. He will not tell you because he knows you are the kind who will not trust it. And he waits until he knows that you can trust it."

She stared at her fingers and shook her head. "Maybe, I will wait."

Jit set the utensils down with a clatter. "Maybe he can wait longer than you."

She stared out the window and traced the outline of the phone in her pants. Was it foolish, she wondered, to hope for something impossible?

Joom Janpong

A MAN TOLD HER to get out of the car. She stood in warm runoff in front of her uncle's house. Rain pummeled her face, stinging the cuts and bruises. The wind forced itself on her and snatched at her clothing. She wrapped her right arm over her breasts. The thing lay heavy in her stomach, and she cried in the rain.

The driveway was empty. She supposed Nokyung was at the laundry. Amnaj asleep at the bar. She'd been terrified, had felt nothing but intense fear and anger. Then she'd gone numb. Cut apart, separated by something raw and focused and evil. To endure the violence, she'd abandoned herself in an abyss of anonymity.

Returning to herself came as a jolt. She looked down. Water rushed around her ankles. This is me, she kept saying. This is me, and I am here. This is me. I am here.

She went fumbling toward the house. No feeling for her uncle, other than this numbness. He was like a stranger. Someone far off and unknown. She imagined him trying to explain to her mother, his sister, what had happened. But how could he explain this sawing pain in her body, this disgusting taste in her mouth. Her mother would never understand. She would never forgive him.

Lightheaded, she wasn't sure she could make it to the house. Distant, it rose like a faraway mountain. She limped past pomelo trees whipping about in the gusts. Rows of persimmon thrashed back and forth. Beneath a loose brick, she found the house key and went inside.

The phone was ringing. She ignored it and went to the bathroom. Her stomach churned. She had to get the thing out. She found laxatives in the cabinet. She brushed her teeth twice and stripped off her clothing.

In the mirror, she examined the bandage, brown with blood, wrapped around her breasts. Another dressing across her belly, large and white with a patch of swirled rust in the middle.

She sat on the toilet. Her legs shook, and she pressed down hard on the thighs to stop them from shaking.

The man who attended to her might have been a doctor. She wasn't sure. Everything had been red and dim. She'd been vaguely aware that he was sitting next to her. He'd adjusted his horn-rimmed glasses and lit a cigarette. She began to choke on the smoke. She was no longer sure. He'd been smoking and touching her breasts. Something cold and moist on her skin. Then a sharp sting and the needle being tugged through the skin, one way then the other. The smoke. She was choking on the smoke. He'd been amused. As he worked, he seemed to think it was funny that she was choking. The cigarette hanging from his mouth was like an insult and also the ash that floated softly onto her skin.

The phone rang like the screech of a wild bird, and she covered her ears until it went away.

She examined the seeps of blood from the scratches on her thighs. She remembered how they got there, and her stomach jerked with dry heaves. Her head felt hot and compressed. She bent over and held her stomach. She had no air. She gagged, fell off the toilet, and grabbed the porcelain sides. Her breath returned with blunt abdominal punches. A voice kept saying, You wish you were dead. She looked around to find the source, to destroy it. But there was no one.

She wiped a string of saliva from her chin. Her back burned. She began to whimper. A flame ignited in her belly. The iron brand. She grabbed her head, the stubble like needles pricking her palms and squeezed it while she screamed above the howl of the wind outside.

He had given her things, the man with the horn-rimmed glasses. Anti-bacterials. Pills for pain. She found them and swallowed. Then peeled the bandage from her belly. They had scorched her with a red-glowing iron. She was afraid to look. Saw it upside down. Saw it charred black and blood red. She closed her eyes. Her entire body began to shake. She squeezed her nails into her palms. She looked down. Whore. Upside down and black and red. The voice again. It told her to die. The mirror. She punched the mirror. Cracked glass fell on the porcelain and tile. She stuck her fist in her mouth and bit down. Blood. A splinter of glass. Then she dropped to her knees and cried. And felt it hard inside. The thing in her stomach, like a dead child, heavy and hard.

The phone woke her. Blood had soaked the bathroom mat. Her stomach convulsed. She rose to her knees and climbed onto the toilet. Closed her eyes while the contents of her bowels gushed out. She fished inside, pulled it out, ran water over it, and carried it into the kitchen. Placed it inside a bowl on the counter.

She ran bathwater. Inching downward like being lowered into fire. The water turned pink, red, brown. She settled at the bottom and went under with her eyes closed.

A distant, dull hum filled her ears. Nearly asleep, she imagined this was a womb. That she was on the edge of something dark and desolate. That she was standing on that dismal edge and hurtling the contents of her mind into the abyss. Things that had happened, who she had been. Relationships, memories. Then a beast came charging, and she collapsed on the edge, wanting to tumble over into it. But he stopped her from going over. He wanted her to suffer and know that he was the cause.

Pushing against the sides of the tub, she struggled against the confinement and broke free. Flew out of the water and brushed her teeth, endured the strangling spasms in the back of the throat. Then refilled the tub and sank back in.

I won't give up.

She heard herself say this. As she listened to the voice, the pain in her body became a sound. A deep and distant sound like primitive drums. Submerged in the safety of the warm water, she recalled the warmth of Thailand, of misty temples in the mountains, of the earthy smell of her mother. She sensed her body beginning to drift.

In Mae Ai, near the Myanmar border, she used to cut paper into dolls. She cut one for a father and one for a mother. Instead of one sister, she cut two. And she cut one for herself. Precise snips made furniture, tables, chairs, lamps, stoves. She used another sheet of paper for a house and made the father move the furniture inside. One day, she accidentally tore him in half, and she pretended he had died in a plane crash. The mother cooked meals on a butane stove and worked in the fields. She was always complaining that no one would help her, but really she was sad because her husband had died. The two sisters were bossy, and they were ugly. But her doll, the one she had cut to look beautiful, was happy, and everything worked out for her. When she wanted a handsome man to love her forever, she cut one out of paper. They took care of each other and kissed when no one was looking.

Her uncle lived nearby then and had introduced them to a woman who had come from the United States. She was pretty with blonde hair and fair skin. She petted the woman's skin as if it were an expensive cloth. She showed the woman her cut-out family, and the woman tried to play with her, but she kept matching the handsome doll with one of the sisters. And this made her angry, and she refused to play with the woman. Her uncle married the woman, and they left for America. And then they broke up. She remembered how puzzled she was. She had imagined her uncle being something like the handsome man she had cut out, and she didn't understand how he could no longer be married to the woman.

Then, years later, their uncle phoned and told their mother to send them to America. They could find husbands. She was so excited, but Nokyung didn't want to go. She was always so plain, never wanting to do anything. She hounded Nokyung and eventually persuaded her. On the flight over, they giggled and dreamed up rich, handsome men who would take care of them. Nokyung might have guessed already what they would find. She might have known. She may even have told her. But she wasn't listening. She was hoping—determined—to find the handsome man that she had once cut out of paper.

She toed the stopper. The draining water tickled her skin and mixed with the throbs of pain. In the empty tub, she lay naked with eyes closed and wondered what she would do next. Wished she could lie perfectly still in the empty tub forever. She would never move. Someone might find her years from now shriveled and lifeless. She sighed and rose from the tub.

She found the medicine the man with the horn-rimmed glasses had given her and spread the cream over the lacerations. She neatly set the bandages on the floor of one of the bedrooms. The gauze snagged the stitches on her breasts. She put on socks and underwear. A large housecoat around her shoulders. She held the phone and stared at the bowl on the counter. She touched-in Nokyung's number, then stopped, unable to focus. Set the phone down and picked up the bowl. The object inside clanked against the ceramic and glinted in the light. She set it down and looked at the phone. What will I say?

The wind howled outside. The rain beat against the roof. The cry of the storm roused the nightmare.

As she relived it, her hands began to tremble. Overpowered by sensation. The sound of machines. The frost of metal. The scent of leather. The obscene gaze of the beast and of what they forced her to do.

Her stomach began jerking uncontrollably. She ran to the bathroom and brushed her teeth. Spat blood into the basin. Stared at a vague, ravaged face in the mirror. A reflection she no longer recognized. The austere head of a wandering monk.

The ravaged face of the storm outside. The beast bore down, and she couldn't breathe through the mindless pain. He had crammed his fat fingers into her mouth and choked her. She'd bitten down hard. He yelled and began smacking her head. She tried to snap his fingers off with her teeth. Half her head had gone numb. He smacked her hard over and over and wrenched the fingers out of her mouth and flung her against a wall. In his rage, he hadn't noticed what she had in her mouth. Before he reached her, before he realized what she'd done, she swallowed the ring. And now it lay glinting in the ceramic bowl on the counter.

She phoned Nokyung. She would know what to do.

Ray Reynolds

He woke in a state of hypervigilance. He heard the sweep of gunfire and felt for his weapon. The ceiling looked familiar. The spin of the fan. The gaslight-style casings. Then he remembered he was on the floor next to the bed. He was not there; he was here, here in his home. The sound came again. A tree limb scraping against the side of the house in a gust of wind. He was not there. He was here, lying on the floor.

Above, on the bed, SevenEight snored. A woman murmured.

He couldn't see Katia but remembered the way she slept twisted in the sheets. He heard her familiar, soft sound as she turned in bed next to SevenEight.

Rainfall pounded the windows. A tree limb combed the brick outside.

The mattress swelled. One of them, or both, were rising from it. He saw SevenEight's elbow, his side of the bed still compressed, and knew Katia had gotten up. A sound like a creeping cat over carpet. She would be naked. A brisk shout of tap water in the basin. The toilet seat going down.

Then a pair of crusty feet swung over the side and hung just above his chest. He closed his eyes. SevenEight might step on him. Something he liked to do for a joke. This time, he planted his feet on the floor and went around into the bathroom. He heard them mumbling at first. Then everything was silent except for the blasts of wind and rain.

He imagined Katia perched on the toilet and SevenEight

on his knees, resting his head on her thighs. She would stroke his hair, that's what she would do, and he'd close his eyes. He could barely make out their voices. The wind, the rain, the whispers of morning. He was certain SevenEight was speaking. Still alert from the sweep of imagined gunfire, he began to pick up the words. She would stroke his hair while he spoke. That was Katia, how she'd do it. Always ready to give comfort.

"You can't understand how we is."

SevenEight's voice. Mixed with the storm, it had become gentle. SevenEight on his knees. A confession at the toilet. His head on her lap. Her fingers slipping through his hair.

"The pain. You can't do it. Can't begin to understand."

Then it was silent. Katia might have been speaking. She might have been whispering. He heard nothing but the sound of the rain beating against the window.

"Terrible and horrible," he said. "And mind-blowing. Adrenalin pumps notched up. Days of flat-out nothing. We be walking around praying we get hammered just soes we could kill something. That bullshit about war and honor? Fuck that. It's about killing. Kill hajj before he kill you."

SevenEight's voice seemed to shake from the bathroom. A lonely echo against the tile. The sound of a man deep in a cave, crying for help.

"Way we be with each other. A blood bond. I let my own family die before I let him die, or any of my squad. That's how we is. And things got crazy. No ups and downs. Both of us, the way we be feeling. There was no fucking way. Couldn't be. But it was. And I already know it. The look he give me."

Katia mumbled something. She'd be stroking his neck, trying to turn the head, so she could look in his eyes. He'd resist, root his cheek into her thigh.

"Unthinkable," he said. The swallowed tone, SevenEight wasn't really talking to her anymore.

Katia's voice finally carried. "Unthinkable," she said.

Echoes from a dark and inaccessible cave.

He lay on the floor and stared at the fan spinning slowly. "Unthinkable," he said, his voice so small that it was lost in the roar of the storm.

Then SevenEight's tone changed. She would be stroking his hair, touching the forehead. She must have asked him to tell her what had happened. She must have because his tone changed. Because he would not tell her. Because no one could ever know.

"When Reynolds brung me in," he said. "When I seen you." He chuckled. A sad sound. "I seen you. Seen how you was, and I got jealous, but also, I thought . . ." He would be staring between her legs at the water in the bowl. He would talking into her thigh. "I thought. I wanted you to save me."

"Save you?"

He lay on the floor and listened to the wind. Cringed as it beat against the side of the house. The ceaseless drone in his ears. He imagined Katia had now looked into SevenEight's eyes. She'd try but wouldn't be able to figure it out. "What do you mean, save you?"

"What else could I do? Adrift in the States. Suspicious, paranoid. Nothing, and no one to trust. All the innocent things—IEDs set to blow. And Reynolds, just like me—"

"He's not just like you." She must have pulled him up by the shoulders. Must have stared into his face.

"Just like me, baby," SevenEight said. "Fucking cored out."

He lay on the floor and listened to the relentless attack of the storm. He closed his eyes and saw the labyrinthine caverns within. Katia would never get it the way SevenEight did. He'd seen the mountains and felt the cold. The moon dust clogging the senses. The snap of bullets. The smell of ammonia when all the fat was gone and nothing but muscle left to burn. The feel of hot brass underfoot. The stink of the shit-burners. And death. The grim rale of the soul bleeding out. He clasped his shaking fingers together.

"And there you was," SevenEight said. "Reynolds brung me in, and there you was. Me, I be wishin', hopin', prayin'. And I seen you. Seen how you was. Certain you could save me."

"Save you? You make me want to laugh and cry. To destroy you."

An image crept in. Mountains rose out of the valley, and the dust stung the eyes. An OP near a town. Locals going about their business. Fear saturated the air. It seeped into the boots. Random gunfire, unpredictable explosions. Fear like fleas crawling on his skin. He brushed it away.

"Save you?" Katia's voice broke with tears. "You stole my husband."

"I love your husband."

"You—but you are cruel."

"Had to make a new man," he said. "Had to. Wasn't supposed to happen. But if I fucking crushed him, then it wasn't real. Gone, like that. Thought I could fucking leave it back there."

The image clawed back. Vivid dreams split reality. He heard a sound. SevenEight rubbing his temples, rubbing his skin raw. He nearly jumped, seeing the raw, bleeding skin of the girl with the orange head covering. She seemed to be beckoning him. Her arm behind her back. He was certain she had a grenade. Certain. But he came closer. He stepped easily from one world to the next. Advanced over the rocky terrain, the cold mountains in the distance, to gaze at the terror in her eyes.

"Never mind," SevenEight said. "You can't fucking understand."

"And this would excuse your cruelty?"

"I don't know." SevenEight's voice trailed off.

He heard the rustle of the shower curtain and imagined SevenEight backing into it.

"I don't know," SevenEight said, "but I feel alive."

The toilet flushed. The shower came on.

He lay on the floor with his eyes closed. Wind smashed against the house. He relived it in wide-screen. A blaring soundtrack. No choice but to step from one world to the next. He was not himself. The mountains imposed on him. The dust forced him. He couldn't stop it. Mackie-Two couldn't stop talking about her, the girl in orange. Those eyes, he said. And you know beneath that garb, she's got an ass built for fucking. Damn straight, hard-ass fucking. They were watching a market. SevenEight saying shit and Slater nearly asleep. Don't let them fool you, Mackie-Two said. They all want a stiff cock. He was pulling his crotch. Shit, she's thirteen, tops, SevenEight said. Mackie-Two looked stunned. Pussy's pussy, man. Fuck's the matter with you? Eyes locked, squaring up. Forget it, Reynolds said. Eyes out. But then Slater got into it. Let's see where she goes. He laughed. Maybe she got a fucking sister. They were strolling along, acting casual, like it was nothing. Ahead, the girl was chatting with her mother. The mother scolded a smaller child for trying to pull her hand away. They bought vegetables and carried them in a patterned sack. The mother seemed to have noticed them and pulled the children close and shuffled away between rows of dried fish and bins of pomegranate. Mackie-Two was scratching his cock through his pants. Hot damn, he kept saying. Hot damn. He had his strut in gear. See that mama's asshole pucker, SevenEight said. She done fucking spotted us. Spread out, Slater said. They were casual, strolling like it was nothing. The family hurried around a corner. Slater jogged after them. Back against an earthen wall, he looked around. Thumbs up. He'd found the home. That night, SevenEight woke Reynolds. He hovered darkly. Let's get us some camel-toe pussy, he said. They slipped out loaded for a mission and found the house. Mud walls mixed with straw. Wooden beams jutting out. Slater kicked in the door. Mackie-Two followed. A man, maybe the grandfather, shouted. SevenEight cracked the man's head with the butt of his weapon. He shoved the muzzle into the father's mouth, forced him to his knees. Big, heavy tears rolled out of his eyes, and he began howling. Mackie-Two was on top of the girl who'd worn orange. Quick man, SevenEight was shouting. Mackie-Two choked her. Banged her head against the floor. Slater took the mother over the table. He kept yelling at the husband. Yelling and laughing. Reynolds checked the rooms. He found the small girl hidden behind baskets in a corner. He dragged her into the main room. His ears pounded with the cries of the girl, the mother, the father. Worried scared they'd be heard outside. The grandfather splayed out on the floor, neck bent, head broken. A pool of blood flowed at an angle toward one wall. Reynolds nearly dropped his weapon. The reddish room surreal, the edges bending and softening with haze. He made for the door. SevenEight shouted, and he stopped. He turned. Mackie-Two had ruined the graceful contours of the girl's neck with a Gerber blade. Had nearly torn the head off. Mackie-Two turned around, an insane grin lacerating his face. The red, glistening penis used up and leaking against his pants. Hot damn, he kept shouting. Hot damn. The sound bored through Reynolds's chest. He was holding the hand of the little girl. She was wailing. Her face, a long smear of running snot. Slater finished the mother, jerked her head back, and ripped her throat with a black blade. He rolled her off the table in front of the husband, who rose screeching from his knees. SevenEight shot a hole in his head. Slater turned to Reynolds. What the fuck you waiting for? He looked at the girl. Mackie-Two buttoned up, still hollering, still strutting. SevenEight said, We're all in this. You got short straw. Do it. Reynolds shook his head. SevenEight raised his weapon. Do it, motherfucker, or I'll waste you. The girl squeezed his hand. She had moist, dark eyes, like wet, black olives.

He heard the shower snap off. A silent moment. Then rain clawed against the window. A shudder of pain when he unclenched his fists.

There had been an investigation. He was sick of it all. He couldn't wait to be questioned. He didn't care. He wanted to die. He thought of Katia and became violently ill. He could never touch her again. He couldn't. He didn't deserve to live, and he was afraid to kill himself. SevenEight had spotted this vulnerability and had taken control. He waited for the investigators. Wanted to tell them everything. He waited, ready to talk. But no one came. No one asked him what happened. Later, he saw an Internet story. The event had been denied.

The phone rang. He sat up and leaned against the bed.

SevenEight came out of the bathroom dripping wet. He walked around the room. "En La Playa," he said into the phone. "Midnight."

The tree scraped against the house.

"No one there. Owner's out. Got it covered. Katia got the fucking key. She let you in. Nothing to worry about."

He felt the bed rail dig into his back. The tone of SevenEight's voice, its snap, its businesslike manner, made him realize that he must have been talking to Dupuis.

"Ring?" SevenEight said. "Fuck the ring. All right, whatever. I'll fucking get it, you goddamn sentimental bastard."

Katia came out wearing a towel. She sat on the edge of the bed.

SevenEight hung up.

"Who was that?" Katia toweled her hair.

"Listen up. Joom got Dupuis's ring. You know it. That fucking thing always on his fat fucking finger. See what you find out. Nice to show up with it. Show-proof my resourcefulness."

"A ring?"

"Yeah, you know what one." SevenEight burst out laughing. "Fuck, girl, you surehell know what one. Your goddamn father's ring. One that Count of Monte Crisco give him."

Katia spoke quietly. "Turbay. President of Colombia."

"Yeahfuck, whatever." SevenEight rubbed his hands. "What a fucking night. All coming together. See that, baby? You find it, and after we done, I get it back for you. Fat ass going down tonight and won't be needing it."

He eased upward from the floor and stood naked while SevenEight parted the blinds. SevenEight was a fool. He might take down Dupuis. He was good enough for that. But a world of trouble would come. He glanced at Katia. She toweled her hair. They'd be after SevenEight. No end to it. And he wasn't ready for that.

Without turning, SevenEight said, "Know that little drive-through? Between the dunes, where they got that Saint Judas statue built up on the tall one?"

He stood naked and cold. "San Raphael."

"Who give a shit? Want your niggerass there at ten. Tonight. At ten."

"Roads'll wash out."

"Make sure your ass is there."

SevenEight craned his head, peered out the window to one side then the other. "Damn weather. But it's good. All good." He gestured. "Take a look at this shit."

He stood at the window with SevenEight.

"See that?"

He saw a woman in a beat-up red car parked on the side of the street.

SevenEight laughed. "Bitch oughta run for it. Fucking storm ain't going nowhere no time soon."

Amnaj Boonngamanong

ALL THAT WAS LEFT was the front window, and he nearly shattered it with the hammer, and he wished he had, such was his fury and desire to put what he'd done out of his mind. He'd waited until the last minute to get this one up. Storms were unpredictable. That's what he'd remembered. Elena, that crazy bitch of a storm, coming toward them in '85 and then cutting east toward the Big Bend, south of Tallahassee. Then reversing course and slamming into the Panhandle. Molly might do that. She might do anything. He put up the plywood from a stack on the side of the building.

Maria arrived to help out. Later Katia. He did what he could before they showed up. The windows on the second story. The ones on the sides. Anything to stay busy. Nokyung hadn't answered the phone. He called the cleaners. Jit said Nokyung was gone for the day. Gone where? She didn't know. He stayed busy. He cut plywood. He squared it on frames. He hammered nails. Just enough to keep the wood tight but not permanent. Maria held the plywood while he hammered. Then Katia arrived. They went inside soaked through, dripping on the floor.

"Have you eaten?" Katia stood at the counter.

He had been busy all morning. He glanced at the clock. "Is it really that late?"

Maria squeezed her hair with paper towels. "Have you heard from Joom?"

"Shh." He heard Katia and saw the look she gave Maria.

"One panel left," he said. "For the large window in the front. But it's late. I didn't know it was late."

Nokyung hadn't answered the phone. She was not at the cleaners. He hadn't called Joom. He was afraid to think about her.

"A few hours until the party." He wiped water from his face.

"No one will come," Katia said. She made hot dogs with guacamole and chopped onions.

"Nokyung should be here," he said, "to prepare for the party. I need to ready the grill. Maria, get the meat, get the pig."

He sensed they were annoyed. Katia fixed food in a stiff manner. Maria hesitating, watching. Katia motioned, get the meat. Maria moved tentatively. They doubted there would be a party. Thought he was out of his mind. He saw that. But Katia should know better. They'd never closed, and they wouldn't now.

Katia carried the plate, set it down. "No one will come."

He bit into the bun. They were irritable. Nokyung, especially. That's why she hadn't answered the phone. Joom, of course. But he'd warned her. He told her not to flirt with that man. She hadn't listened. So, it was her own fault.

"Of course they will." He wiped his mouth. "My best customers will be here. Nails. The Mexicans. What else can they do but put up roofs and drink?"

"They don't drink much."

"They drink enough. They'll be here. Get the meat."

Nokyung would bring trouble. She'd tell her mother, his sister. Manee would call. She'd be hysterical. It's her own fault, he'd say. He'd say it calmly. Matter-of-fact. She flirted too much. I warned her, but she didn't listen. Manee would be hysterical. It's her own fault, he'd say. Maybe yours, too. He saw that he might say that. Put the blame where it really belonged. My fault? she'd scream over the line. Maybe you shouldn't have let them come, he'd say.

"No one will come," Katia said.

He put the hot dog down and glared. The way her eyes glanced about. She was nervous. Something struck him as not right. But he didn't have time to think about it.

"They'll come," he said, and grabbed up the hot dog. "Go help Maria."

My fault? Manee would scream again. She'd scream several times. That was Manee. Always getting hysterical. Can't have a discussion with a hysterical woman. He'd have to end the call quickly. They have no respect, he'd say. They don't listen. He'd hear a groan of disbelief. Nokyung has no respect? Her voice shrill with hysterics. Nokyung is plain, he'd say. Plain with no chance. But disrespectful all the same. She attacked me, did you know that, P'Manee? He'd hold the phone away from his ear. He'd have to. Manee would be screeching.

He ate the hot dog and watched Maria and Katia unpacking the meat and running water over it. They were chatting, occasionally glancing in his direction. Maria annoyed. Katia determined. Complaining about the party, he was sure of it.

Even as a child, Manee would screech when she could no longer stand to hear something. You are supposed to protect them, she'd say. How she got to this, he didn't know. Can't talk with hysterical women. They hit you from all sides. He'd wait until she was silent. Then he would sigh. The sigh would be long. It would be deep. It would convey sympathy for her struggles. That would do it. The sigh always stilled her. He'd shrug and say through a long sigh, It's up to them. There would be more silence, except the silence on an international call would be like an echoing hum, like chanting monks heard from afar.

Maria was shaking her head. Katia wagged a finger. Something struck him as not right, more than complaining. Katia was scolding Maria. What could she have done?

Maybe they should come home, Manee would say. Yes, he'd say, maybe so. Can you get some money for them? she'd ask. Yes, he'd say. They'd hang up. He'd deal with the truth later.

He set the phone on the table. Finished the hot dog and wiped his mouth. Katia and Maria had turned away from him. But he was certain of what he'd seen. What had passed between them. He'd take care of it in a minute. He opened the phone.

Nokyung answered.

"You should be here helping out. Where are you?"

"I'm coming."

He heard the wind shaking her voice.

"The party will start soon. You need to be here. And bring Joom."

He heard hesitating, faltering sounds in her voice. The wind, he assumed.

"I'm coming," she said.

He hung up.

"Katia. Over here."

She left Maria, whose eyes, he noted, fixed strangely on the counter. Her lips in a pout.

"What's up with her?"

"It's nothing," Katia said, sitting. "I got on to her for working too slow. Esa always needs some prodding."

Katia laughed, but he sensed the laugh was for his benefit.

"You gave her money. Why?"

"Oh, that." Katia laughed again. "A loan, that's all. Tips aren't as good with this storm."

Something more, he thought, though he couldn't figure it out. Maria stood on the verge of tears. And Katia laughed like it was nothing.

Katia touched his hand. "Listen," she said. "I have a favor."

He looked at her.

She nodded toward Maria. "She's in a tight spot. This storm and all. She's got some things to move and can't find anyone to help. I'd do it. But it's big things. So, maybe you'd . . . I can open the bar, get the party going. Wouldn't take long. An hour, maybe two."

"That's it?"

She smiled. She patted his hand.

"Por su puesto." She nodded. "That's it."

Katia Molino

THEY CARRIED THE PIG out last. They set it on newspapers spread out on the counter. The pig had an expression of amused curiosity that made her think of one happy year long ago when she was a young woman, a time of fresh orchid blooms and the skyward sway of palms against the rich Colombian sky. But it was also a heavy-hearted time, a time of loneliness and longing for the return of Camilo. He promised when he went into the jungle with the others that he would return. He promised, and she made the love in her eyes so plain to him, and he went into the jungle under the weight of that promise, and—there was no use to think of it. She wished now only for work.

She pushed aside ribs and steaks to make more room. It was too much. She watched Maria taking out knives and noticed that her gaze fell on Amnaj. He stared at the rafters, absently biting into his hot dog.

"Help me," she said, separating rib portions with a knife.

Maria hesitated. "Do you really think there will be a party tonight?"

"Like this," she said, slicing between the bones. "Your fingers like this. Your thumb here."

She'd get the hang of it. But if Joom and Nokyung were here, they'd be nearly done. Nothing against Maria. She worked hard. No one had a better eye for spotting customers who needed refills. And she never complained, though they gave her the toilets during clean up. Spirited but never rebellious. But she truly wondered as she followed the tiny girl's hands dissecting the meat, would tonight do it? Would it wreck her?

The corners of her mouth became heavy as she watched Maria handle the pig roughly, as if she wanted it to feel pain. She recalled the night they took Joom. Maria's reaction, the hand of ice, the black, vacant stare.

The poor girl was in a tight spot. Had no idea what SevenEight had in store for her. In part, she was cold toward the girl. Better now to feel the crush of the hand she'd been dealt, and she owed nothing to Maria. This bitterness, she searched for its root and located it in the death of Camilo—at least she believed he was dead, for she never found out what had happened to her first husband. And there was that pig sitting on the counter with its smug grin as if taunting her by its own death, revealing how the crust surrounding her own heart had become thick and impenetrable.

Yet all these months she'd kept a watchful eye on Maria, and it must have been, she realized at that moment, that they were all alike, and there was no one else to turn to, no one with the brute force of compassion to save them. She would have to get Maria out. Maria could not be a part of what was going to happen.

A surge of determination rose in her breast, and her mood then brightened. She could stop it. SevenEight would beat her to a pulp. That was true. But she could save Maria. She took up the work and made a plan. The ribs in her hands were cold and slimy like the task, but it had to be done. She turned with hope toward Maria.

"You know *el gusta de ti*," she said.

Maria paused. "Who?"

She indicated Amnaj with a nod.

Maria glanced at the table, her face tight and hard.

"Don't you know?"

Maria looked at the meat and shook her head. "No, not him. He's *muy viejo*."

"*Tonta.* Of course he does." She heard her own voice rising with girlish excitement. "You're blushing, *niña*. You know it's true. Why do I have to tell you?"

Maria pursed her lips and sawed through the ribs. "No," she said. "Not for me."

She touched Maria's arm. "I'm telling you, he does. Maybe you are too busy to see how he looks at you. How he finds a way to be near you."

Maria looked up. Their eyes met. She could not hold the gaze and looked away. This was not going as she planned. She'd hoped to arouse Maria's interest, play on her desire, if she had any, for admiration. But her intense, dark eyes were unbearable.

"*Qué?* Why do you look at me like that?"

Maria dragged a lock of hair behind her ear. "You really don't know, do you? Who he has an eye on."

She lowered her hands. A slab of cold, raw meat numbed her fingers. But her face felt warm. A flow of heat from her mouth to her breasts. She turned away and washed her hands. She dried them with a towel and glanced at Amnaj. He was on the phone and seemed upset. She breathed slowly and checked herself. She had to do this. She turned back to Maria.

"Take him home with you tonight."

"Amnaj?" Maria shook her head. "He's not for me."

"Tonight. Take him home."

"Hurricane party, remember?"

"No party tonight. Understand? Do as I say."

Maria pursed her lips. Something frantic in her features.

"I have some money for you." She nudged Maria. Skin icy as the meat. "Take him home with you."

Maria's mouth parted. A look of protest, of disgust. Her head began to sway. "You want me to . . ." She blushed. It was not a blush of innocence but of rage. Her words seemed to crumble in her mouth. "Dormir con él."

Maria would soon explode. She knew it but kept coolly detached and pushed it. "There's money for you."

Maria began shaking, her lips trembling.

"Oh, Jesús Cristo. No, no."

She blocked her so that Amnaj wouldn't see them and become suspicious.

"You must do this, Maria. There's money for you. I've protected you—"

"Protected me? This is—"

She snatched Maria's arm, held it tight, and leaned into the quivering girl.

"I'm sorry, mija. Don't reject this. Think where you would be. Think if you would be better off with Flaco. That's what awaits you."

She clutched Maria's arm. Saw how her eyes darted, how they became enflamed at the mention of Flaco. She decided this was a useful wedge.

"That's right, niña. He would sell you for nothing. He and that runt, Joel. You see how they come on to you. What do you think they want? To love you? No, no. They want putas. That is their business. You'll be flat on your back with your legs spread all night long. Who do you think stops them?"

Maria began to weep.

"Here." She held out the money. "Take it."

"It's SevenEight, isn't it?" Maria wiped her right cheek with her left hand. "That's who it is. It's not you. It's him."

She caught Maria's hand. "Take it. Take the money. Take him home with you."

"I won't do it."

Maria's tone was hard, but her hand began to soften. She pressed herself close, gave Maria a pillar to lean against. "Mija, I know, I know. Hush, niña. I'm sorry. It's hard for you. But you are not going to get a husband here. You may as well know that. You are adrift, and you must take what you can get. To-night, it will be him. Tonight, you will take him home."

She released the money into Maria's hand and watched her fingers close over the cash.

She heard Amnaj's voice, her name.

"Clean yourself up," she said and went around the counter.

She sat with Amnaj, smiled, and patted his hand. Her phone rang. It was Nokyung, and she sounded upset. She stood, deciding it'd be better if Amnaj didn't know.

"It's Reynolds," she lied to Amnaj. "I better take this."

Amnaj nodded. "We'll be outside putting up plywood. Maria!"

"Just a minute," she said into the phone. She waited until

Amnaj and Maria had gone outside.

She had to sit down as Nokyung told her of Joom's condition. Dios mío, she whispered into the phone. She could not believe what they had done. Then her attention shifted as Nokyung described how Joom had taken Dupuis's ring, her father's ring, and she saw a chance to get it back, but Nokyung's voice scared her; it was filled with rage, and she spoke of revenge. "Nothing stupid," she told Nokyung. "Come to the bar. Yes, I'll be here. We'll figure this out." She listened to the shallow breath on the other end and imagined Nokyung gazing at her sister with wet, red eyes and shaking with the force of vengeance. "Come to the bar," she said again. "Promise you will come."

She hung up. The windows were dark, covered with plywood. She heard hammering. Then it ceased. Then a car engine. Then. They were gone. She felt loneliness penetrating her body. It would be all right. Maria would manage. A crash of thunder shook the bar. There was still a chance. She slid open the phone and pressed a number.

Nokyung Janpong

RAIN SLASHED THE STOREFRONT window. It came at angles, shiny and sharp as needles. Traffic seemed to float over the road. Headlights bobbed like Loy Krathong candles floating down the Kok River. But these grim drifting lights would not carry away her troubles. Lightning flashed. The wind knocked hard on the door and sent moist drafts inside. The gray turbulence reflected her worries, her fear of what would come.

She wet-cleaned a satin dress. Arranged it on a hanger. Moved to the next one. Since hearing from Joom, she'd wanted nothing more than to leave. But she avoided asking Jit for permission to go, avoided rousing her curiosity. The impulse became an infestation of drumming urgency. Still, she bit her lip and resisted.

At last, she finished and said goodnight to Jit and dashed outside. A blast of wind knocked her off-balance. She leaned into the roar and crawled into her car. She merged into traffic. The radio spoke of evacuation areas. The bridges were closing. The center of the storm was offshore and accelerating. Landfall would be later that night. The beat of the rain, the beat of the wipers, the beat of her heart; they were all the same. She raced through a changing light and passed a truck. At a stoplight, she rummaged through her purse and found the card and turned it over. She dialed the number.

"Nokyung?" Stickleback's voice was steady.

"Joom is on the island," she said, killing the quaver in her voice. "I must get to her."

"Can't do it. Seaside Bridge is closed."

"You can help me. I must go to her."

They met at the bridge. Near orange and white barrels, Stickleback spoke to officers in rain gear. Yellow lights flashed at intervals. He came to the window.

"We'll take my SUV."

She shook her head. "I must have my car to get back."

"I'll wait."

"No. You can not. Please. Can you get me over?"

He had his hands on the rim of the door. He leaned in and seemed to study her, to see the minute twitches she felt in her cheeks, the tension of her brows.

"Move over," he said. "I'll drive."

She squirmed across the console into the passenger's seat. He climbed in on a surging tide of rain and then drove past the barricade. Wind rocked the car going up. He radioed for a pick-up on the other side. She noticed the ring was not on his finger. She decided to say nothing and looked ahead. They rode in silence. On the other side, he got out and leaned inside.

"The roads are washing out. Avoid deep or standing water. Go slow. Go steady. Don't rush. If something happens, stay put or get to higher ground. Call me."

The steady look of his wet face gave her assurance. He had passed this feeling to her, she realized, and it reminded her of the stone impression of the Buddha's footprint she'd seen near Chiang Mai. It was raining then, too. Yellow, unopened lotus flowers lay about. She'd heard the legends. Imagined the

Buddha flying to this spot and landing with such force that it made a deep and permanent imprint in the rock. In Stickleback's face, she saw those images. Serenity. An unspoken promise. She began to roll up the window. He removed his hands. She stopped and, not looking at him, said, "Thank you."

"Be careful." And he stepped away.

Her uncle's house rose like an island from a sea of flood water. She slipped off her shoes and cuffed her pants and went barefoot to the house. The door was unlocked. She found Joom sitting on the floor in one of the bedrooms. She was trying to wrap the bandage around her chest but looked confused and helpless.

She sank to her knees. Her stomach began convulsing. A greasy, bitter taste coated her tongue. She pressed her lips tight to prevent herself from crying. She touched the remaining tufts of Joom's hair. The rest had been shorn. Joom's eyes began to fill with water.

She held Joom's shoulders and whispered, "Oh, ตัวเอง ตัวเอง, let it all out."

Bruises the color of storms covered Joom's body. Seeps of blood stained her naked breasts. The stitches were crude like wire ribbons where the nipples had been.

Not now. She refused to fall apart. She held her breath and then felt it shudder through her lungs. She acted quickly.

"Let me do that." She took the gauze from Joom's hands.

Joom lifted an ointment from the floor. "This first."

"Is it too painful?"

Joom produced an orange bottle with a white cap. "Painkillers." She could barely speak. "Yes. Painful. A thousand stings."

She applied the ointment and wrapped the gauze over Joom's breasts. Tears fell on her fingers. She looked up.

Joom's downturned mouth trembled. "I want to go home."

She patted Joom's arm, scooted closer, kept a steady rhythm on her arm. "Hold on, ตัวเอง," she said. "Hold on."

"It hurts."

"I know it does. Hold on."

"I want to go home."

"I know, ตัวเอง. Hold on."

"I can't stand it." Tears rolled down her cheeks and splashed on her bare thighs. "I want to go home."

"I know. I know. Hold on."

She tenderly turned the bandage around Joom's chest and taped it on the side. She held Joom's hand. She wasn't sure what to say. Rain beat on the roof. She patted her hand and gazed at her face. Touched her wrists, touched her elbows, touched her shoulders. They were quiet, and they looked at each other. Joom's lip tremored suddenly. Nokyung caressed her fingers. Rain beat on the roof.

She helped Joom slip into the housecoat. Felt herself grimacing as Joom brought it together gingerly across her breasts.

"You are adrift in this madness, จุ๋ม, but you must hold on. You must."

"I just want to go home."

"There's nothing there. Nothing better. Nothing you can do. Hold on."

A shriek of wind stirred a howl of rage in her breast. She rose, blind with malice, and went into another room. Joom couldn't see her like this, not in this brutal state of unsighted fury. She collapsed against a wall behind a door and called Katia and told her what she had found. At last, she controlled her breathing and returned with a shaky smile that nearly collapsed when she saw Joom rumpled on the floor like a castoff doll.

Joom wiped her face. "Does Uncle know?"

She shook her head. "Not a thing. Don't tell him. It will be worse." She took Joom's hand. "We have to go. The island is evacuated."

She found clothes and helped Joom into them.

"I want to respect Grandmother," Joom said. Her expression was exhausted, a thing collapsing into itself.

"Quickly."

They lit thin yellow candles and knelt in front of the altar. She felt Joom bend low to the ground, while she looked deeply into the framed photo of her grandparents, deeply into the eyes of her grandmother, and then she closed her eyes and kowtowed. The grit of the floor nibbled at her forehead. She'd meant to keep her mind pure in this moment but found herself drifting, trying to figure out why this had happened to her sister. Nothing sensible showed up. Unless Joom had been cruel in another life. Unless she had done something horrible to cause pain, and now it was her turn. She could not imagine it. Refused to believe it. Her thoughts drifted as if through curtained rooms. An image of her grandmother sitting with her legs straight on the floor. Old, and no longer able to walk, she still smiled with unrevealed joy and touched them when they brought the evening meal. After their terrifying crossing through the rice fields with the food, they would cling to her. Her voice covered them, soft like summer wind. She had made them feel safe. They would beg to stay the night. Her voice, even as it refused them, carried in it the gentle reminder that she was not her body, she was not her mind. She was nothing more than a way of experiencing the world. The path of life, she had said, is a stick drawn through water. The words were confusing. They remained confusing throughout her life. But she had never forgotten them. Or the comfort they brought.

She helped Joom from the floor. "We must go. I told Katia—Oh, where's the ring?"

They went to the kitchen. Nokyung dropped the ring into a plastic zip bag. Stuffed it into her pocket.

"Katia has some idea," she said. "We must go to En La Playa."

They splashed to the car. Lightning struck across the dunes. The trees shook with violence.

Katia Molino

THE PIG SWEATED ON the counter. Thawed, its curious expression wilted, its jowls sunk with malaise. All around, a comfortable, quiet murmur settled like dust in a sealed room. But outside, the wind screamed as if it carried within its heart an unrelenting pain that nothing could heal.

She lugged the pig into the cooler. Then the ribs and steaks. While she was in the back, she heard the wind shove against the door, and she thought it had forced itself into the bar. But when she came out, the door was closed, and nothing but brooding, airless shadows kept her company.

A glance at the clock. The evening crowd had yet to arrive. They weren't coming, anyway.

But he would; he would come.

SevenEight had set it up. She would add an enticement. Her fingers trembled as she pressed out Dupuis's number. A deep breath.

"Plan has changed," she said. "Ten o'clock. Yes. I've got it."

That was done. A wave of calm spread downward from her chest. She laughed softly and dialed Nokyung. "He's coming," she said and hung up.

"Who coming?" A voice knelled from the shadows.

She dropped the phone with a weak cry. She knew the voice but not like this. She spun around. Jimmy Nails stood next to her.

"You startled me." The counter mashed her hip.

"Who coming?"

He seemed unbalanced without a pool cue.

"No one. We're closed."

"Bullshit."

As he passed under the track lights, his hooks turned a knife shade of blue.

"Really," she said, looking for a way out. "We're closed. Amnaj will be back soon."

Nails smiled. "Don't think so. Saw him heading out with Maria. Ain't look like he in no hurry."

He stepped into a clearing between tables. Began to shadow box, the hooks cocked, striking the air. The step quick and graceful. He made noises—*ja ja*—with each jab. The pumped expression of his face, she'd never seen it before. He seemed transported to another realm. No longer in the bar but under arena lights. A boisterous crowd all around. *Ja ja.* Then he turned, the feet quick, the hooks balled at his chest. She saw how he looked at her, how the shanked eyes narrowed, the bellows of his nose expanded and contracted. His lips wet with a killing instinct.

"Damn, I'm feeling good." He seemed surprised at his own feeling. "Like I could go me a few rounds with a son of bitch if I could find me a son of bitch that need a little ground-and-pound."

He bullseyed a glance. "Know anyone like that?"

She didn't move. She listened to the roar of the wind beating on the door. The furious drone of the rain.

He shouldered in close. She looked at him. He smiled. "Could take your pick, couldn't you? Shithole place like this.

Just about anyone. Like punching fish in a barrel."

She held onto the counter. Told herself to remain calm. Felt her torso bending against the counter. She followed his eyes. They searched her face. She looked away. Stared at the door to give him nothing.

"You'd tell me, wouldn't you? If it was that cocksucker, SevenEight?" He jabbed past her ear and laughed. "Yeah, you'd tell me. He fucking you, and you just don't give a shit about him. Ergo—that be Latin for so—must be somebody else. Who?"

She shook her head. "No one." She inched along the counter. "I'm closing up."

He blocked her way. Another jab past her ear. A sound like a striking match. He came in close. Breath like oiled leather. "Yeah, you gonna tell me."

She turned but felt the cold metal of the hook catching her chin, pulling. She glared into his eyes.

"I am telling you," she said. "Nothing's happening. What you heard. What you thought you heard. Was something else. Some place I have to be. Now, I must lock up."

She attempted to move. He drove his leg between hers, pinned her to the counter.

"You'd be amazed," he said, and she felt the tip of the hook against her temple, "what this thing will do. Take an eye out as easy as popping a zit. Pop. Gone."

She struggled as much as she dared. He ground himself between her legs. She spat at him. Saliva slid down the stony cheek. He grinned. The cold metal dug into the corner of her eye. "Pop!" She jerked, but he crushed her against the counter.

"Must be something important," he said. His teeth brown,

broken. "Worth losing an eye over. Not SevenEight. Not that cocksucker. Somebody else." He smiled, he chuckled. "Dupuis?"

She glanced at the floor.

"What I thought."

She expected him to release her, but instead, he thrust his leg deeper into her crotch and needled her eyelid with the hook.

"In '87," he said, "punk name of Mike Staub figured he'd mix with me. Staub the Blob, I aliased him. Punk called me out. He sure did. Mother, fucker called me out. What I do? You already know it. Could feel my fists smashing his ribs. His skin folding around my hands. Like I be deep-fisting some bitch pussy. That deep. You don't mess with me. Then bam bam bang. He look like a mountain lying there. A sweaty, fucking mountain. Punk shoulda stuck to eating french fries."

He released her. She stumbled against a barstool.

"Get out," she said.

"Going." He spun around, jabbed the air. "Going." Turned at the door, and the rain doused his shoulders. Wind carried his voice. "Gone."

She collapsed against the counter, caught her breath. Things were out of hand. She had wanted to keep Amnaj out of this. Her knees trembling. She clutched the counter. Not by herself. Couldn't do this by herself. She needed him.

Steady once more, she flipped off the lights, leaving on only the amber one near the register and the red one over the call shelf.

Outside, she could barely stand. The wind had flipped the

grill. Plastic bags, milk jugs, and glass bottles tumbled over pavement. She leaned into the door and locked it.

Nokyung had said on the phone that she'd hoped to cross the bridge before it closed. Maybe she wouldn't make it. Maybe she'd be alone.

Wind-tossed, Katia staggered through the rising water toward her car. The door slammed shut on her leg, and she rubbed it while the wind rocked her inside.

Maybe he wouldn't come. But he had to. Get there, and bring him back. All she was thinking.

Maria Castillo

She stood in the gray light of dusk. Soaking wet, swaying in front of room seventeen. The heavy curtain of the wide window flickered with the amber shades of a man she wanted to love. Flickered in melancholy light, dim as her hope.

Amnaj had been surprised to learn that she had, in fact, nothing to move. He'd looked at her as if he'd been the butt of a joke.

Katia was ignorant. She had assumed that Amnaj desired her. But she'd never encouraged him. Never raised a warm hand or doe eye of interest.

Katia was blind. They'd arrived and had shaken off the rain. His only interest was in whether she had beer. Maria fetched one, but he was already asleep on the couch. She spread a blanket over him and went out.

She gazed wistfully at the shadows moving behind the heavy curtain of room seventeen. Separated by wall and world, she shivered, bathed in cold water streaming from her hair. Over her eyes. Around her nose. She licked it from her lips.

A stubborn thought pushed against her forehead. Hard to believe. She could not accept that Joel sold women.

The light inside flickered warmly like the dream that had cheered her since she'd met him. She imagined a life together. He as husband, she as wife. A candle's whispered incantation. And honeyed words for honeyed skin. A shawled head tucked under chin. Breath softly thieving across his chest.

Fuck her. Fuck Katia.

The dream she'd stolen. She couldn't let it go. Refused to believe a diablo lay beyond the door of room seventeen.

She would keep it no matter what. Keep it by letting him live. As long as he was alive, so was her dream.

The wind howled like a pack of coyotes. She knocked on the door of room eighteen.

Flaco, opening up, plucked a cigarette from his mouth. He wore dirty jeans. Underwear flowered upward around a bare torso.

"Come in, mamacita," he said, leaving open the door, and turned away.

She closed the door.

A bottle of tequila in a sullied palm. A ditchwater stain dull on a shirtless back. When he spoke, she heard the brutal desert in his voice. The disdain was evident. She was not a person.

He laughed without looking. "I knew you'd come for my big cock, pendeja," he said. "A whore, and nothing else."

She slipped the revolver from her pocket and waited for him to turn around. When he did, he licked his lips.

"For my grandmother," she said.

"Fuck your grandmother," he said.

She shot him in the face.

Ray Reynolds

"Closing up, Ray," Eileen said. "One for the road?"

"Hit me."

Eileen poured coffee and dumped the rest. "Bad out," she said. "Guess you'd rather be home."

He pressed the lid snug. Stood by the counter.

"Duty calls," he said. "Get out of here, Eileen, before it gets dark and nasty. And drive safely."

Buttoned rain gear, he pushed out the glass door.

The cruiser turned onto the nearly empty street. Initial flood surge ran over the asphalt. At the station, he'd heard the storm would be more windy than wet, but there'd be enough of both. He patrolled his area of responsibility. Warn the party dumbfucks to evacuate the island. A short list of indigents and handicapped. Make sure they were out and safe. He scanned the streets, the boarded businesses, particular attention on vans and cargo vehicles. Later he'd check on Maria. Like other illegals, she'd hole up and hide. Wouldn't know to get off the island. Would be afraid of being caught. He'd see that she was OK. He glanced to the left. There's one. He pulled into the parking lot of a used coin shop and rolled up next to a hatchback.

A skinny man in a yellow bucket hat bustled outside with boxes.

He lowered the window. "See your ID?"

The man looked stricken. To put the man at ease, he

donned the concerned cop face.

Nothing happening here, anyway.

The man owned the shop. "Coins," he said, indicating the boxes.

"Anything good?" Easy with the voice. The man was jittery.

"Some rare finds," he said. "Real surprises. Things you never expect."

"Bridge closes in thirty minutes." He set the cruiser in gear. "Best be going."

The man nodded. A sheet of rain cascaded over the brim of his cap.

Later, he pulled up, window-to-window, next to Heebner in the parking lot of a beachwear outlet. "How's the saddle feel?"

Heebner looked a little pale. "Done with the day and pulling a half-shift. I'm exhausted. Spent half of last night securing my artwork. Going to grab a little bunk eye and back out tomorrow."

"You might as well go home and come back with your broom. Ain't nothing happening in this shit."

"Wife's got the kid up in Enterprise, safe and sound, so I might as well stay."

A gust of rain sprayed inside the cruiser. Reynolds wiped his face. Through the moisture he saw Heebner yawn. The guy was pushing it, trying to prove too much too soon. But Reynolds knew the feeling. Man's world's a show-proof world. You're nothing without it.

Reynolds put the car in gear. "Take care." He rolled up window.

As night fell, he thought more about the meeting with SevenEight. He'd hoped the roads would wash out. He radioed in a downed power pole. Recorded names and addresses of a middle-aged couple who were staying put for the body count later.

Lights already out in some areas. He could just make out the hulks of businesses and homes on the sound side of the island. Deserted mostly. Eerie with the absence of light and people. He turned onto the main beach road and made way to the San Raphael monument.

Headlights siphoned off by darkness, he waited. The cruiser rocked in the wind. At times, the force of it made him think the vehicle would be thrown up onto the dunes. Rain, heavy then light, in noisy squalls. He stared south, stared through the slick patterns of sliding water on the windshield. The more he stared, the more he saw the storm as a raging beast rising from the Gulf, a black entity crawling over land surfaces and flogging everything in its path. He felt choked by it.

Headlights flashed in the mirror. SevenEight slid into the cruiser with a howl that could have been the wind. "Shit, that some badass something out there."

He glanced in the rearview. Astonished to see another set of headlights. Instead of going past, the headlights went dark. Someone had tailed SevenEight. Then it made sense. Dupuis was no fool. He saw how it had happened. SevenEight couldn't keep his mouth shut. It got back to Dupuis. He'd sent a thug to restore his props. He glanced at SevenEight. He hadn't a clue. He could tell him, but he wouldn't. The thug had two bullets. One for SevenEight. He didn't give a shit about that one. The other one, though. That was for him. The bullet he'd been waiting for. All at once, he felt relieved.

"Fucking went by International," SevenEight said. "Fucking boarded up. So, you gonna drive."

"What?"

"Nigger, you got the fucking cruiser. The goddamn right and the goddamn power to be out in this shit."

It didn't matter. The thug was coming. He felt him stepping over the wet sand. First SevenEight because he was shit. Then him—because he was there. That'd do just fine.

SevenEight threw up his hands. "Fuck!"

"What is it?"

"Left my goddamn nine in the fucking car. Shit. Ain't going back out there. Get it for me."

"What the hell—"

"Go on. You in the rain gear. Get your fucking ass over there. Front seat."

Wind nearly yanked the door from his hands. Didn't matter. The thug would cap him first. Though he'd hoped to watch SevenEight die. He went around the car and stood face-to-face with the thug. But it wasn't a thug.

"Maria?"

"Tell him to come outside."

In her hand. Small, black, barreled.

"Tell him."

He opened the door. "Get out."

"Fuck are you doing, nigger?"

He held the door, preventing SevenEight from shutting it.

"Get out."

"Gonna get out all right. Get out and fuck your ass all over."

He shoved his way out and then started laughing. "What this bitch be doing?"

Maria shot him in the head.

SevenEight's head snapped back, shattering the laugh on his lips. His head smacked hard against the vehicle. Then knees, face, sand, down, dead.

He slipped the revolver from Maria's hand and replaced it with his hand. Then the wind resumed howling as if nothing at all had happened.

Jimmy Nails

His nature was to go against the elements. The unrelenting force of the wind slugged his face. He leaned into it. Dared it to take him down. Thick as steel, his chest squared against the blasts. He controlled his breath. Kept it cool and steady. Rain like pussy jabs glancing off the head.

He left En La Playa. Hadn't gone far. Slogged through rushing streams of water. His feet soaked. Hands cold. The sensation took him back. He stared at the hooks. Water like beads of sweat glinted from the metal. He had no hands, yet he couldn't deny the cold that gripped them.

Not long now. He hadn't gone far. Down the road. A boarded-up convenience store. Under a wide awning, he wedged between a commercial ice box and a propane cage. Crouched and waiting. Wouldn't be long. Wiped the hooks against his shirt. Couldn't believe how cold they felt. The last time he'd felt this cold was in New Orleans. Night had fallen. Streetball beneath a tall blue lamp. Got into a fight. He was always in a fight. His father told him, when you're balls-to-balls, watch the eyes. No pussy shoving. Strike first, and hit hard. They learned not to look at him. Look, and get hit. His father taught him, and he taught them.

The rep stuck like a tune in the head. They made room where he walked. He and Dean Gray soon became best pals. Gray, known for the care he took with his paddle, made a show of taking it to woodshop and drilling holes in the pine blade.

"For all you sissy screamers," and made sure everyone saw it.

Dean Gray was a fat son of a bitch. Wide mouth. Thick rows of buttery teeth. A laugh that shook down to his blobby ankles. All that trouble, all those times in Dean Gray's office, and he never got a single lick. The paddle was cradled in a small stand like a trophy on Dean Gray's desk. Something to look at and piss in your pants over. But he never got a lick. Dean Gray saw something in him. No other explanation. Took him one afternoon to a boxing club. Total immersion. All that tangy sweat and blood. The creak of the heavy bag chain, the swivel of the speed bag. Barbershopping about punching and pussy. He was in heaven.

Crab took him in, showed him what to do. They called him Crab because he once fucked a bitch with crabs. Even after he was cured, he couldn't shake the sensation. Was scratching all the time. Even when he didn't have crabs, he had crabs, and they called him Crab. Man had no teeth. He was young, and he had no teeth. He liked Crab right away. A voice like buttermilk. Smooth, thick, and sour.

Wasn't long before he was somebody. Everyone knew it, and no one messed with him. A match in Baton Rouge, another in Brownsville. Fights in the club, where his father would tell him to strike first, and hit hard, and Dean Gray would tell him not to turn into a sissy screamer. That expansive feeling of seeing his name, Jack Samsom, on the marquee board lifted him like one of the stilt-walkers in the Jingle Parade.

"Be in lights one day," Crab told him. He tried not to think about it. Got his nose busted in Mobile. Played it through right to the end and hammered the guy with seconds remaining. Afterward, he absorbed the sound of the clanging lockers, steam rising from his skin, blood flowing from his nose. Wouldn't say a word. Just savor the smell of his life. While Crab unlaced the gloves, he counted the bruises, as if counting badges of honor on a soldier's chest.

His opponents went down, and he climbed the ladder, rung by rung. An undercard match in Las Vegas. He took one in the mouth. Ringside, he told Crab. Crab said, spit it out. The tooth clattered in a squirt of blood at the bottom of the plastic container. Crab shoved the mouthpiece back in. "You'll never catch me, kid. You don't lose 'em fast enough." After that one, he grabbed space. A month later, Crab found him at home. "*KO* is calling you 'Jammin' Jack.' Here, listen up. They say you a 'brawler like a slow storm system.' How you like that shit? Ever hear of Arturo Hernandez? No? You will. Fucking Arturo Hernandez. Can't fucking believe it. Next Tuesday. Want you to meet the man. Next Tuesday. All about it."

Tired of crouching, he sat in the water. Didn't matter. He was soaked, and it wouldn't be long. A plastic trash can rolled across the street. A beat-up red car went past. A woman driving. A man in the passenger. Barely made them out. Something told him they were scared.

He had a girl with a red car. Her name was Troya Owens. She was two years older. They met at Club OGs on Marais. She had a four-year-old. Didn't know who the father was. Too much candy blunt. That was all right. Boy was funny. Made him laugh. Guess she got tired of him. He missed the boy. He could find out but didn't want to know. Drank malt liquor with Ario, her brother. Dumbass name. Selling dope.

Lucky to be out, or alive. Dumbass name for a dumbass. "He make money on you," Troya said. They were good then. The boy sleeping on the couch in the other room. They were naked in bed. His cock slimy and soft. Mouth smoke green in the bathroom light.

"What you saying?"

"Ario," she said. "He put money on you. Everybody do that. Know you beat the shit out of them. You the best thing ever happen to him."

He hadn't known.

"All over," she said. "People bet on you. Whether you win or lose. How many rounds. Anything. You're good for the economy. Don't be like you don't know."

She played with his balls. Yeah, he knew. Maybe he didn't care. Just no one had said it like that. No one gave it a name, made it real. All about the fight and nothing else. He knew, and he didn't care. Then hated being everybody's ox.

"Clean me up, bitch."

Down the body like warm honey. Mouth, a swarm of bees. He lost himself in the dim, green glow of the bathroom light.

Tuesday. He walked to Two Sisters on Derbigny. Arrived late. Crab selling him to Mr. Stint. Lawrence Stint, who had it all arranged. They were drinking coffee. He ordered water, no ice.

"Fucking Arturo Hernandez," Crab said. He was beside himself.

He shrugged.

"Title shot," Crab said. "Fucking Arturo Hernandez. You'll kill him."

Crab had a new set of teeth. Polished acrylic, aligned perfect as ringside seats.

"It's all set," Crab said.

In September, he'd fly to Miami to fight for the cruiser-weight belt.

"Pay-per-fucking-view," Crab said. "The works." Crab was beside himself. "Fucking Arturo Hernandez."

Afterward, in the parking lot, he said, "You got money on me, Crab?"

Crab flicked his tongue over the acrylics.

"Fuck you," Crab said.

He declined a ride and walked back to his apartment. The air hung limp with the stagnant smell of piss.

In August, he ran into Ario at the laundry. His shirts were drying. He watched them spin. Ario came up. They went outside. Ario's forehead was beaded with sweat. He looked to be using more than selling.

"Need to know," Ario said. "Any truth in it?"

He must have looked stupid. He gazed at the sweat on Ario's forehead.

"Come on," Ario said. "You can tell me. You cashing in? Word you going in the tank in number eight. You got your reasons. I ain't asking. Just wanna know where to put my flow."

He stepped away. One punch. All it would take to kill the guy.

"Who talking?"

"Shit, Money, who ain't? Word spread like a bitch's legs."

One punch. That was all. He returned to the dryer and

took out his shirts. They were still damp. He stuffed them in a duffel and pounded away down the sidewalk. Fuck 'em all.

He heard an explosive crash and looked past the ice box. A pine tree twisted and fallen over the liquor store across the street. Almost time. Not long now. A gust of wind drove his head against the plywood. The punch. Just like that.

Miami was a mirage. Sweltering. He could barely breathe, let alone move. From the locker, he heard the sound in the arena. Inhaled slowly and exhaled with a noise like a speedway. Crab wrapped and laced him, layered his face with petroleum jelly. Then left him alone with "five minutes."

He emerged from the tunnel and floated like trash through a sea of rowdy people toward the ring. The crowd was manic. Arms waving like the antenna of a hundred insects trapped in a jar. Bells rang. Announcements echoed in the hall. He filled the arena. Saw himself moving toward the ring. A slow storm system. Black and roiling with unpredictable strikes of lightning. He couldn't tell how long it would take, but he knew the outcome. Hernandez on the canvas. Blood seeping from his mouth. The sweaty froth of the punctured countdown. He saw it with the certainty of his own existence. They came out and squared up.

Hernandez danced. He liked to dance. That was his style. But he was steady, not a clown. He respected Hernandez for this. He watched the eyes. Like fighting in the streets. Balls-to-balls, like his father said. Strike first, and hit hard. He watched and waited for the eyes to show fear. The precise moment he would take him down.

Hernandez was a pussy shover. Spent two rounds testing it out like he was making sure it was real. He waited and watched. Hernandez came out jacked in the third. Quick jabs to the head. Lefts to the body. He stared hard and showed no fury, no weakness, no pain. A slow storm system coming on the horizon. Powerful. Inevitable. He held back, let it ride, the leg muscles like rockets ready to rip. In the fifth, Hernandez attacked the ribs, went for the whiskers, pounded the gut. With twenty seconds to go, they fell into a clinch, and he held Hernandez up. His breath dying like the calm before the KO. The man was exhausted. Is this it? All you got?

The bell rang. He walked back to the corner. Crab swabbed cotton, applied cold metal, and kept saying, "Take him down. Down." He watched Hernandez in the corner, searched the eyes, saw how limp the lids were, sagging like old tits over his eyeballs. He spit into the bucket.

Back on the canvas, he landed a blow that sent Hernandez against the ropes. To a knee. A hollowing cry from the crowd. But he wasn't ready yet. He hoped Hernandez would regain his footing. The ref hovered, underarms stained, bowtie bent. Hernandez gloved the ropes, pulled up, struck the gloves. Again, the little dance, the feet jigging the hot plate. Hernandez came back with wild, scattered punches. He could have taken him, he was so open. The bell rang.

He saw defeat there in the battered, purple eyes. Nearly over. He saw it in the limp turn. The legs going fast.

Is this it? All you got?

Hernandez collapsed on the stool. He turned his back. Crab was waving, hustling him over. Grabbed his shoulders. "Don't throw it. Don't do it."

"What the fuck you saying?"

Crab dug into a cut over his eye with a cotton swab.

Eighth round.

He glared at Crab.

"That what you think?"

Crab shook his head, wrung out a smile. A convincer to hide the doubt. The acrylics blinding in the arena lights.

"Title's why I'm here."

He was shouting, spitting blood at Crab.

"Fuck you, fuck you."

Crab wouldn't look at him. He stuck in the mouthpiece.

"He still strong," Crab said, still not looking. "Don't be fooled."

He felt heavy. For the first time saw faces in the crowd. Anonymous, ravaged faces. All of them scum. He was their ox, and they didn't give a shit about him. Just how much he could make. All hope riding on the crooked back of his willingness to take a dive.

Hernandez went right to work. Dull pain in his ribs. Then a lingering sting in his eye. Sweat flooded the sockets. Blinded by the swarming blur, he'd lost the eyes. He knew where to look but could no longer see them. Saw a woman ringside. She was dressed in blue sequins. She was laughing gaily. A chain of silver around her neck. He'd lost focus. Lost the eyes. Then the punch blew his head back.

Crab said, "You'll get another shot," and unlaced the gloves.

Four men came into the locker. "Get out," one said to Crab.

They locked the door. One eye shut with blood. The other

followed blurs moving toward him. Pinned to the table. He could still hear himself screaming, the same piercing sound as the saw. He heard the hand fall to the floor, and he began to cry. The other with no noise at all. Just before he passed out, he saw one of them peering down. A slight man in horn-rimmed glasses. A cigarette dangled from his mouth. He opened a bag and said, "Don't worry. You'll live."

The wind howled. He looked up. Rain splashed his face. He rose from the concrete to punch the ice box. He stopped. He needed the hooks. Felt his stomach churn, felt an urge to vomit. And took a deep breath. It was time. Time to get there and take care of things. He kicked the ice box and strode out into the storm.

Ray Reynolds

"Why?" Once they settled inside Maria's car.

Wind roared outside, but he was stilled by the silence under the fabric headliner. Primitive features, the uncomprehending look of a child. A clean, wet face—and smooth.

"I followed him." A cold shudder in the whisper. Key, tight in her fist.

He looked down. The gun cold in his lap. Like a block of ice.

"I didn't ask you that, Maria."

She turned. A strand of hair clung to her nose.

"Everything is OK now?"

"This is serious, Maria. You can't—"

"I know what he was," she said. An outline of face—the rest cavernous in the darkness. "What he did to Katia and wanted to do to me. What he did to you."

"Yes, but—"

He felt her wet hand. An assured squeeze. Then she told him about Flaco.

"Jesus Christ, Maria. You just can't—"

"It is done," she said.

He rubbed his forehead and looked out at the dunes, black and formless in the raging night, black and formless like the body of SevenEight, already taking on sand.

"OK," he said. "Let's get out of here. I need to think this through."

She started the car and then turned.

"You don't have to come," she said. "Your wife waits at the bar."

Maria knew so little. Much less than she thought. It wasn't as simple as returning to Katia. He had no feeling left. Nothing to do with her. Nothing to do with SevenEight. He had a disease of memory. A terminal haunting that would not let him rest. He gazed through the darkness. Saw in the dash light the vibrant bone structure of Maria's face. The wet shine of her eyes. She felt relief, he guessed, or fledgling hope. A promise that could arise only from innocence.

"No," he said. "That's—never mind. Drive to your place."

Down the deserted highway. Sheets of sand across the road in the high areas and waves of water in the low. She told him that Amnaj was asleep at her apartment. What had happened was easy to imagine, but he didn't ask, and she offered nothing else. He stared out the window, thinking about what to do next, feeling the numbed layers of his skin. They passed a convenience store. A figure huddled against an ice box. "Dumb fuck," he said aloud. "Got no place to go." He decided to be anonymous and picked up Maria's phone. "Guess I'd better call it in."

Maria was silent. He saw the concentration. The way her tongue darted over her lip. It'd been a long time since he'd cared what someone else was thinking.

The headlights, striped with rain, revealed the shells of the driveway, the bending wood of the mailbox, the toppled planters, and the wet patchwork of the concrete walls.

She rushed inside. He followed.

"He's gone," she said. "I was supposed to keep him here." She looked in the bedroom and came out tangling her hair. "Katia told me to keep him here. He was asleep. I was supposed to keep him here."

"It's all right," he said. "Sit down. Take it easy."

"No," she said. "How can I? He was asleep. Right here." She pointed to the couch. "There is his beer. He wanted a beer, but he fell asleep."

To the couch, an arm hesitating on her small shoulder. "Shh," he said. "It's OK."

"I need to call Katia." She twisted up. "She needs to know. She counted on me."

He led her back down. "It's OK," he said. "We'll call her. But we have to talk now. Get things straight."

"We have to call her."

"We will." He rubbed her arm. "You were here the whole time." He caught her hand. Held it firm. "You were here."

"Here?"

"Yes."

He saw that she was confused. Did not understand that he meant to save her.

"You were here, and he fell asleep, and when you woke up, he was gone."

He looked into her eyes. Watched them dart. Frantic tongue on the lips. Unrest in the mind. He recognized the infiltration of panic. She'd killed two men. You could do that only by cold separation, the brutal denial of life and emotion, or by immersion into the heat of passion, hysterics, or madness. She'd walled herself off, but already the demon was coming savagely through the walls. She needed most now to know that no one would hurt her. He rubbed her arm. Brought her close. Her tense thigh persuaded by touch to loosen. Then careful fingers on her cheek, faint strokes on her skin.

"You were here," he said. "You were here."

He imagined this must be what hypnotists do. Lull their subjects with warmth and whispers. He watched her lids flicker, felt heat return to her face. In the tone of spells, of murmured incantation, he spoke in a voice that sealed her mouth and closed her eyes. Her shoulder planted against his chest, and he felt in the moisture of her skin the exhaustion seep from her body. Felt it through the clothes. And last of all, fighting against fear, her eyelids went limp, buckled under the weary weight of sleep. He spread a blanket over her. The curved, yielding frame beneath his arm. Something in the dreamy distance of her face. A break in the clouds. A kind of daylight. His arm on her hip. And he watched it take form. The dim shape of hope.

Katia Molino

SHOVED TO THE SHOULDER, she fought to keep the car steady on the washing, windswept road. Power utility trucks in hunkered-down crouches, their buckets pulled close like the claws of crabs. She went past slowly, glancing up. Inside the cabs, behind wet glass, an elbow and a hardhat, all in deep sleep, awaiting the aftermath and the job of restoring power.

No bars on the phone. The resolve that had raged in Nokyung's voice, and she imagined Joom nearby, teeth set, hands forged into fists—the idea sketchy at best, lifted from smoldering torments of heart—and who knew in these matters what was right and what was true—things grim and ruthless and would not yield, she was certain, even if Amnaj could be found.

Second thoughts, and pressure in her temples. A moment of panic had sent her out to find Amnaj. She needed him. That's how it had announced itself after Nails's visit. But, did she? Blunt pressure above the ears. Would he get involved or play middleman, as he usually did—and how then could the thing be stopped? Keep him out, keep him safe. A palm to her head, pushback on the relentless pressure, and then it was decided. Keep him out, keep him safe. And she would take care of everything.

Wind shoveled sand over the glass. The wipers scraped with irritation, and she nearly missed Maria's apartment. It was behind a two-story house painted sea green. Cinderblock, square, and flat. A rutted shell lane between mailboxes on wooden posts. The posts on the ground, and she had missed them. She backed up and turned down the lane. Maria's car parked against a shattering, shaking fence. A drop of orange light behind the curtain.

The screen door clattered on the concrete block, and she pushed inside. The altar grabbed her eye. The Virgin haloed by a small lamp. Shadows on the couch.

Reynolds, a finger at his lips. Maria lay across him. Her hand curled at her mouth. Tiny beneath the blanket, infantile. A socked-foot protruding.

"Where's Amnaj?" She pulled a chair close.

"What's up?"

"He was supposed to be here. Maria—"

"She's exhausted."

Breath flowed warm through her nose.

"Where is he?"

He glanced down. Brushed a lock of hair from Maria's cheek.

She was surprised by his gentleness.

"What's happened?" she said. "Something wrong?"

In his hands, the slant of body, he was different. The sweep of a vigilant eye. Then he looked up.

"Don't you know," and his hand never left her shoulder, "we're all wrong. Battered, broken, bruised," and his hand walked her parapet arm, back and forth, and his gaze returned to the simple, napping shape beneath the blanket.

Sunken below the surface, she realized, he had vanished into the past, merged with it, and no longer knew the difference.

"I need to find Amnaj. What did she tell you?"

"He left when she fell asleep."

"Where?"

"She doesn't know. She was asleep."

That wasn't right. A beer stood full on the table. The Virgin with palms together at the heart. Face to the side, eyes averted.

"No," she said. "Your cruiser. How'd you get here?"

The forgetful motion of his hand, a thing lost on her shoulder. And Maria's cheek wet on his thigh, her lips rippling in comfort. Then she saw that he didn't know what he was doing, didn't see his own hand, or the compassion he believed he'd lost.

Then the wind shook the cottage and brought her back to purpose. She leaned, sought his eyes.

"You must tell me, Ray. Where?"

"He left, and she went to look for him. She was rattled when I spotted her on the road."

"Rattled?"

"Yes. Left the cruiser and drove her here. She's exhausted."

"So, where is he?"

He shook his head and glanced away. Once more drawn to the serene palm, his placid fingers. They reached beyond the cuddled form, and she felt herself also soothed and drowsy, but he did not mean it for her sake but for Maria's, and she made a tiny sound, a burble of contentment, and Reynolds, though he did not seem to know it, responded with warmth.

Then she connected it.

And sat back, bunched arms beneath forsaken breasts.

Noticed the photos in gold frames. Parents and a grandmother. They stared out with homely expressions. Eyes so simple they would be jarred to look upon the danger surrounding Maria.

Attention back to Reynolds. He was different. Not the man she'd loved, and not the man who'd come back from the war. She didn't know this man.

"You made me proud," she said. "You know that, right?"

He nodded.

"I loved you," she said. "You know I loved you."

"I know."

"You came back broken."

She expected his head to sag, but he continued to look at her.

"I blamed myself," she said. "That's what I thought. That I wasn't loving you enough."

"It wasn't your fault."

"But I blamed myself."

"It wasn't your fault."

"Anything for you, Ray. Anything to bring you back."

Tears gathered, and she sniffed them back. Even a different voice. No longer the one that had adored her. Then Maria made a terrifying sound, and a hand came clutching from the blanket. He captured the hand, consoled it. And only the sound lingered—round, plaintive, and devastating. He bent his head. Shh. But it was not his voice. Shh. It no longer belonged to her. Shh. The voice now belonged to Maria.

She looked away. The eyes of the parents and the grandmother. She knew the look. What they wanted most in the world was for their child to be safe.

As she gazed at the altar, she became aware that her right hand played with the wedding ring on her left. Turned it. Tugged it. And then it was off. Pinched like poison between thumb and finger.

A disconnecting click, the sound of a dropped call, the ring on the table. The rich, gold circlet abandoned and quickly losing heat. She waited. Gave him a chance to tell her she was wrong. Waited and watched his hand on Maria's shoulder. She knew then he would not speak.

"Where will you go?"

"Southwest," he said. "Mexico. A beach on the Pacific."

She forced a smile, and he looked at Maria.

"Home."

She stood, bracing against the chair. "I need to find Amnaj."

He nodded.

Knees weak, she turned at the door.

"Take care of her."

He nodded.

Outside, palming tears from her eyes.

ธรณีนี่นี้เป็นพยาน

THEY ATTACKED WITH KNIVES. Pounced like tigers. Struck like rattlers. The wind drove him inside, his body blown across the threshold, and knives sharpened to fine edges ripped his skin. Knives in his chest, his neck, his shoulders. And the wind came with him, a cyclone of fat and flesh. A large shadow screeching in pain and with terror. Grasping, kicking, clawing, he turned over chairs. And the howls of the wind pierced their ears as the blades pierced his face, his legs, his back. Down, down to his knees, and a serrated edge tore across his throat. A squall of blood covered them. And they licked it, his blood from their lips. And rolled him onto his back and stripped the clothing as if it were skin. They worked in silence. Buckets tall as their knees. Grooved knives, straight knives, boning knives, carving knives. They had a circular saw. They had a cleaver. And they worked with diligence and speed. From the outside in. The noise of the circular screeched when it hit bone. And his feet came off. Wrists severed, and the floor thick with blood. Slippery with fat. They tore through his windpipe and plucked his head like a rotten fruit from a tough vine and tossed it aside. The head tumbled once and came to rest on the floor against a stool. They sliced his middle, and the entrails bubbled up and floated like a snake on water. Ferociously, they snatched his wet heart from the sundered chest. Held it meaty and red and dripping, and a great primeval cry arose from the floor and passed through them chilly and dry. Then working in silence, working joint by joint, they carved away muscle, scooped fat, and sawed bone. They hollowed his trunk. Spleen, kidneys, liver removed like goodies from a treat basket. They pared cock from groin. Working downward, knife to balls, it came away as a set, and they laid it tangled and ground it into the floorboards. Answering their laughter, the storm battered the building and then, unexpectedly, hushed, as if it, too, feared them. And they looked at one another in bewilderment. Afraid to speak. The slick floor, the cupreous smell of blood. The pieces, clumps, mounds, and parts. Then the fine whittling work of erasing him. Paring, dicing, shaving—into flakes, chunks, and negligible waste. Dumped and poured into buckets. The lights flickered. And then went out. And they vanished in darkness.

Solemn beneath the smooth, black night. Standing and stunned by the silence. The stillness of the air. As if they'd stumbled into a grim yet serene underworld in which only they existed. And cast an eye upward. An eye that saw stars. Stars like tears. Tears that made them feel moist and small. The beauty—staggered by awe, yanked into transcendence—they gazed at the beauty. And had they a shake of time, they would have stood for eternity beneath this tearful sky. But they didn't have time. The Gulf's ceaseless beating, its froth, its churn, and endless swelling and breaking reminded them that time they did not have, that no one had time, and the storm's eye would soon close. Buckets lifted, they slogged across the parking lot single file. Crossed the road where wet sand squeaked beneath wet shoes. Marched across the shell, and the buckets bumped their legs, and the contents sloshed with ire that clutched the chest. They climbed the steps of the pier whose pylons had buckled under the storm's onslaught and pounded over the slippery wooden slats to the end. And chum spilled from the buckets into the churning waves of the Gulf of Mexico. Down it went, down it went. And they turned without glancing at the stars, for they knew if they lingered, they would never leave.

Jimmy Nails

"I CAN CLEAN MY OWN goddamn hands," he said, pulling away. Joom made a face. "You don't have hands. You have hooks. Give them to me." And she unbuckled the harness, and somehow it just wasn't right.

Fuck it. Ain't feeling sorry for her. That'd be easy. Her face, a rough sea of black and red bruises. Not a stitch of hair and just going on about it, and suddenly that frightened him, and it wasn't right. That she'd care for him when she needed it more.

"What about that?"

She paused and looked up. "What do you mean?"

"I hear. I see. You know what I be saying."

She shrugged and drew off one of the hooks. "Be still, and let me work."

Shrugged like it was nothing. Acting all badass, and he'd show her the pain. So, after both hooks were off, he thrust the stubs at her face. "How ya like it? Pretty ugly, huh?"

What'd she do next? Grabbed 'em hard and ran a stiff finger down the scars. "There, that's ugly."

She turned to clean the hooks, and he turned away, didn't want to see her face no more, and listened to the storm outside now blowing from the southwest. The eye passed on during the night. A few more hours, and it'd be gone. Northwest and grinding through Alabama, clipping the corner of Mississippi, and on up into Arkansas. But over for them. And that sinking feeling, and life beside the point.

The howling beyond the plywood called for one last fight. He nearly choked when it struck. All the rage shook out. And what was left? Nothing. The headstone: He shot pool with the Mexicans. That's a goddamn life. He stared at the scars.

Back in New Orleans. Couldn't show his face. Everybody talking 'bout he done throwed the fight. A razor, the first attempt. Done it in the tub. Troya come by to do his hair for old times' sake. Fuck her. The scar above it? Been so drunk, he couldn't cut straight. Felt goddamn foolish in the hospital. And the long one? That whole fucking mountain range of scar tissue? Gone in deep that time. And what was it? His father's birthday. He stanched the wound and called an ambulance. Each time it got easier, though. Fear of death diminishing like some big ol' ghost deep in the bayou. He needed a new surrounding, and come east. Fucking Florida Panhandle.

Midsummer rang at him like a bell. En La Playa. A complete unknown in a bar where English was a second language. Talk about the fucking holy grail of vanishing acts. Way too good, and now the vanishing looked even better.

A swim in a beautiful sea, that's how he'd go.

Beautiful.

He was ready, and a hand touched his shoulder.

"Turn around." Joom worked the straps back on, positioned the hooks.

He could still see her hair, the way it had fallen down her face, had billowed on the shoulder. Unbearable, that's what it was. The slope of her cheek, the bend of her neck. He looked away, stared at the floor, and hated what he felt, like she stood for something. For what he'd lost. His hands, his fight. And brought the thing he'd long abandoned back in the buckling of straps, her thin fingers girding the hooks.

No, he'd go to the water. Nothing else left to do. Dive deep and swim until worn out.

She tugged the hooks, "There," and went off to clean.

Outside unnoticed, easily forgotten. The pier shook dimly in the first etchings of dawn, gloomy and gray. The wind challenged him right off. He jogged away from the pier, throwing out meaningless punches. Across the road and staggered over gravel that gave way in large chunks. He found a running rhythm and over shell and stone pounded up and over a sliding dune. And evading the grabbing sea oats sprinted across the wide flat beach. Ran and punched, dodged and spun. Led with the left, countered with the right.

The waves crashed on the shore. Curling, they came with mean lips and white teeth. He raced for it, head on and without fear. Saw it across the ripping tide. Beautiful and final. A great swallowing. Go inside and down down down, fighting and furious to the bottom and close his eyes and rest his head, and it wasn't so bad.

Like a beacon of light, it caught the corner of his eye. Slower, faltering, he stopped, and a surge of sudsy water rushed over his shoes. No fucking way.

It was bobbing on the waves. White and blue and impossible.

The wind leaned in strong, and he pushed back. "No goddamn fucking way."

The water swirled black and cold, tore his legs and beat his body, and he struck it, reaching for the chariot that spun and dipped and weaved in the foam. And not far now. A hook's length away. And the bursts of metal on plastic spurred the effort, and there was a rope, a twine of blue, and one spanning prong secured it, and the leg muscles burned red in the froth, and with it fastened to his chest, he bore the cooler to the shore.

Inside, the toddler was a smear of water, blue cheeks, and soggy clothing.

He reached down—the hooks—and pulled back. The kid looked up. Not afraid, not crying, not ashamed. Cold. Wet. And more than that. He looked deep into the kid's eyes and followed the gaze. Followed it to the pink spill that stained the gray wall of the horizon.

"I see it," he said. "I see what you see."

He lifted the kid. Took it up in his arms and latched it to his chest.

"I got you." And his voice swirled in the wind.

The kid didn't cry. It wasn't afraid. He talked to it as if it were. To soothe his own fear.

He heard someone calling. A speck, far off, and she was running. The wind knocked her down. She scrambled up and ran. Coming steady and prevailing against the force set against her. Certain as the sun, now clawing through the gray and lighting her with a sheen of gold, and it tore him up, and then the kid lit up, and it was like they was twin stars, the girl running over the beach and the kid clinging to his chest, twin stars bustin' up the night.

Joom Janpong

SHE FELT THE WIND ride up the back of her shirt and knew instantly Nails had gone. And she was afraid to turn around and sought her sister.

Nokyung was standing with a bucket and a jug of bleach. "Go to him."

"What for?"

"Why do you stand there? I see it."

"What do you see?"

"ตามไปซิ ตามไปซิ."

Frozen. Arms limp. And her sister's hands like fire on her shoulders. Then she faced the door, and he was gone, but she'd known it before she'd turned. The wind, it had crawled up her back, it had told her. And she was afraid.

"Go, go."

Nudged, guided, then outside, running. A shadow slipped down the dunes, disappeared among sea oats, and went after it fast and over the road. The wind drilled deep, snatched her clothing, shredded her face. At the top of the dune, she saw him and knew that he meant to vanish beneath the waves. And she was too far away.

She hollered, and the wind scooped up the sound and dumped it. Down the side, wet shoes sticking in the flypaper sand. Ran and shouted, and the wind slapped her to her knees. But she was not giving up and rose out of it and ran on.

He turned, a racing path along the shore, a line she couldn't reach. And the pain beneath her ribs, and the black burn in the pit of her stomach. He dove into the waves, but he would not go down, and a spark of hope fired in her lungs, and she sprinted, mouth open, filled with rain, and then he was gone, vanished beneath the roiling, black surface.

Then the air felt charged, and in the distance, a pink wet glimmer. And he rose like a rock from the water, and she saw what he held.

She pulled him up. By the shoulders. By the arms.

He thrust out the child. "Take it."

She pushed back, head shaking. "No." She held on to him. He held onto the baby. "No," she said. "It is your fate. It was meant for you."

She brushed away the tears and cradled a hook in her hands. Brought it to her lips and kissed it.

Derek Stickleback

Molly had not been as bad as Ivan. More like Frederick, damagewise, and he turned the SUV onto the barrier island's main road. Massive white trucks lined the shoulders, and workers in helmets rode buckets up to repair electrical lines. The pier had held. A few buckled pylons midway out. He gazed at the blue sky. Seemed like forever since he'd seen a sky so crisp and blue.

He felt suddenly grim. Some bad business during the night. Earlier he'd seen Reynolds's abandoned cruiser. An aimless friend, and what could he do? Reynolds had left the vehicle—or he'd been taken off. And next to the cruiser, a body. Soggy, sand-covered, and dead. He had a hunch.

Mixed feelings about his destination. He looked at the sky. Something good in all this. A nice morning sky.

He drove past a hotel, where crews with chainsaws cut palms from the cabana and blew sand from the parking lot. People were strong.

He passed Eileen's. Plywood in stacks on the side of the building. She'd seen Reynolds.

"My last customer," she said.

"Told me to drive safe," she said.

Didn't know anything else.

He slowed where a section of the road had been washed away. He flashed his badge at a worker who pointed to the left shoulder. Shells crunched beneath the tires. Gripping attention, the left hand turning the wheel. Could hardly believe the sensation. As if the hand had been bound with iron for years and had suddenly broken free. He looked at the blue sky. Then the left hand. Something good in all this.

He turned into the parking lot of En La Playa. Trash cans like buoys on a listless sea. Out of the car, he stood listening to the sounds of the Gulf washing over the sand and the hum of the generators on the side of the building. A large sheet of plywood, half-down, covered the front window. He went inside.

His nose burned from a stinging odor. The houselights were on, and it felt awkward, out of place. His eyes adjusted, and he couldn't help smiling.

Nokyung behind the bar. A look of surprise.

He steered across a slant of sunlight. "What is that godawful smell?"

"Very big storm, Detective—"

"Investigator."

"—very big mess."

She set a cup on the counter. "Coffee?"

He nodded, but he was looking around, wondering what had needed such a thorough cleaning.

She poured a cup and poured a second.

"Now we have coffee together," she said.

He smiled. Took a sip.

"Your uncle?"

"Is not here."

He leaned, elbow to counter, and looked over the floor. "Spotless," he said. "Amazing what you can do with a good cleaner."

She was hard to read. Her lips were long and thin and seemed to be working over something.

"Doesn't matter," he said. "It's Katia I wanted to see."

"Not here," she said.

Nervous? The way her lips plied over one another, the way she hadn't sipped the coffee. And she was blushing. Her eyes darted from register to door to table. Then down to her fingers. Of course, he reminded himself, there were cultural considerations. How did a Thai woman act when she was nervous or afraid or in love? He didn't know. He focused on her eyes and decided to go deep.

"SevenEight was shot last night."

He studied her eyes, watched for a flicker. The faint hint of recognition.

"On the beach about a mile from here."

He left out that Reynolds's cruiser was there.

"Looked like he was meeting someone."

Her eyes drifted over the counter as if looking for crumbs to wipe. She sighed.

"You don't seem surprised."

"Why should I be?"

"Well." But he didn't know, and he waited.

"He is mean," she said. "He deserve what he got."

Hard to read. A different angle, twisting the question.

"It's my job," he said. "You understand. Someone said something. Maybe you heard it. Maybe you know something."

She didn't. He knew that. He wasn't sure what he'd hoped she would do. Trip up, confess—or assert her innocence.

He spread his hands flat on the counter. "Do you?"

A pained look flashed in her eyes. Then anger.

"Am I your suspect now?"

He backed up, held up his hands. Then smiled. Lifted the cup.

"Don't take me wrong," he said. "Not you. Of course not. Thought you might have heard something. That's all." He sipped. "You make a good cup."

He talked about the storm for a while. Things he'd seen. The damage, the repairs. He asked how she'd managed.

She told him she was at the bar all night. No hurricane party, after all.

Together they pictured Amnaj out in the storm cooking the pig and laughed.

"A couple of chuckleheads," he said.

She became serious again.

"What is it? Chucklehead?"

He explained, but she didn't seem to understand, and he excused himself to go to the bathroom. Above the urinal, someone had etched a woman on all fours. Huge breasts. Scribbled ink for a crotch. Written above, Joom likes it. An arrow pointed where. A penknife had been used, on closer inspection, to carve the image, and the brutality of the hand that held the knife was evident in the rough outline sliced into the wall. That brute was ubiquitous, and what was he, pissing in the urinal below the caricature of Joom, but an un-guarded step away from that brute and the loss of humanity, and wasn't he better than that, or not?

He sighed. Glanced at the floor and felt his gut wrench. He shook and zipped. Then tore a towel from the dispenser.

He bent down. The coagulated spot was brown. A maroon rim. He wiped it and stood up. His gut, still tossing, told him the story. "Fuck," he said. Stood looking at the floor. He'd find more blood, he was certain. But not today. Images from the morning news. Nails holding the Cooler Baby. Joom, black-eyed and tenacious, by his side. He felt sick. Trembling palms embraced the cool rim of the sink. No, not today. The blue sky. The nice morning air. And Nokyung behind the counter. A good cup of coffee, a laugh, and all that he wanted, right there. Nails had plucked the baby from the sea. And a memory flashed in the pale light of the bathroom. He'd fallen into a well when he was seven and believed himself abandoned, until several hours later, a large, sweaty man hoisted him out and his last strong memory of his mother, later that night, tucking him in bed, telling him, "This poor man cried, and the Lord heard him and saved him out of all his troubles." He looked at the brown spot on the paper towel, closed his fist around it, and dropped it into the trash. Then, he washed his hands.

Nokyung refilled the cup. She seemed annoyed or impatient. Or nervous. She wanted to work, and he was holding her up. He sipped and watched and wanted to know more. But he closed his eyes first and prayed that Nokyung would say the right things, and he would give her the edge.

"Dupuis has gone missing," he said. "His wife called, worried. Have you met her?"

Lips turned down, eyes wandered. An absent shake, a slight shrug.

"Her name's Sorana," he said. "Pretty lady but real torn

up about it. You can imagine. Eyes red and wet and draining off the emotion—what would you call it? Anguish, despair? And she's certain Dupuis's dead. You always think the worst. Poor woman, a stranger in this country, and who knows what she had to do to get here. And now—it's a real shame when you think about it—she's lost her anchor, her hope."

Nokyung stared over his shoulder, bored or detached. He'd need to put it in her lap.

"Can you imagine the hurt," he said, "the awful sorrow, that she, Sorana, his wife must feel?"

Then her eyes shifted, and he felt the intensity of her irritation building, the high-powered drill of her gaze. The exertion to unlock the fastened mouth.

"Maybe," she said, her voice, grim as the grave.

The air was stifling. He rubbed his forehead.

"Not that I give a shit about Dupuis," he said, "but I wondered—him missing, SevenEight dead. Any connection, you think?"

She shrugged. "Maybe Dupuis shot SevenEight."

He sipped and pretended to ponder the idea.

"I don't like how you act toward me," she said suddenly. "Is this what you mean by coffee? All these questions?"

She turned away. Something on the call shelf. He had meant something else by coffee. Now he'd upset her. And what he'd found on the bathroom floor. He'd already decided. It could wait.

She turned back and pointed at his hand.

"Where's your ring?"

He held up the hand and looked at it as if he'd never seen it before.

"I told you," he said, resting it on the counter. "I'm not married. I woke up this morning and decided I would never wear it again."

"I don't believe you."

"And maybe I shouldn't believe you." He sloshed coffee on the counter as he stood. "Maybe you know more than you let on. Maybe you know more about SevenEight, more about Dupuis. More about. All of this."

She hadn't moved. Jaw set, brow stern. The lower lip a muscle of resistance.

He breathed in, out, set the cup down, and softened his tone. "Maybe."

She wiped the spill.

"Maybe not," she said.

He shook his head, turned the cup by its handle, and gazed at the brown spinning brew.

"Maybe you know how I feel."

She flattened the damp rag. White on walnut, it lay like a semaphore whose message could not be decoded.

"Maybe I am going to complicate your life," she said.

He read fear. Plain and prominent in her eyes. Read it and read between it. She would hate him if he continued. He smiled.

"We should have coffee sometime," he said.

"We are having coffee," she said.

He laughed.

She smiled.

"Away from here," he said, looking around. "Away from all this."

She bounced against the counter. Her smile turned skeptical.

"Now you trust me?"

"As much as you trust me."

"Now you are being chucklehead."

Nokyung Janpong

"A dune was there, wasn't it?" Joom pointed to a flat, open area.

Nokyung took Joom's hand. "Now it wants to be a dune here."

They locked arms and crossed the street.

The sky was clear and blue. The Gulf of Mexico washed green and quiet against the white shoreline. They stepped over broken palm, plastic bags, and driftwood. Found a place midway between the dunes and the beach and sat in the sand.

"There is a party at the bar later," Nokyung said.

Joom smiled. "I won't go."

"ตัวเอง, Uncle will be angry."

"I don't care." Joom stretched her neck back, turned it round. "After we gave the baby back to its parents, after the reporters went to them, I stood so close to Jimmy Nails that I felt as if I were attached to him, and then he told me I had no shoes, and I looked down and saw I was barefoot, and we started laughing, and then we walked to a store and he bought me a house shoe and some sock."

"I think maybe he is good to you because you are good to him."

"Do you think so?" Joom pulled her legs to her chin and spoke through her knees. "He invited me to his place today, and I will go. Do you think I should, ยูง?"

Nokyung slid her hands beneath the sand. She felt a cool

sensation up to her wrists. Then she sighed. "ตัวเอง, do you remember why you wanted to come?"

Joom laughed. Her face was mottled with black and green bruises. "We thought we would find husbands."

"That was you. I never did."

"Why did you come?"

Seagulls zipped through the air, alighting on beach and pier.

"Because you wanted to come."

"Because of me?"

"I saw the hope in your eyes, the way you went on." She lifted sand. Let it slide between her fingers. "Maybe you influence me a little. Make me feel what you feel. But I knew there was no hope."

"Like Pa," Joom said. "Practical."

"Yes. But some part of me wanted it to be true. So, I told myself I would come to protect you."

"I wish you had not."

The water sparkled as it rolled onto the beach.

"But I am glad I did."

"I have made such a mess of things."

"No, ตัวเอง, you have not. Maybe it is me who is foolish."

"You? I cannot believe that."

"You are like Maria, จุ๋ม, or the Mexicans. Brave enough to dream. But me? What does Uncle say I am?"

"Plain."

"Yes."

"Hopeless."

"Yes."

They laughed.

A white bird with a black head and a red eye strutted through the waves at the shoreline.

"Sometimes you go on," Nokyung said, "because there is nothing else to do."

"But it all turned out so bad," Joom said.

A fat, brown pelican glided past in defiance of its awkward body.

"Do you remember when we respected Grandmother?"

Joom nodded.

"What came into my head is what she used to say when we complained. Do you remember? She used to take us by the hands. And she would say, อยู่ใต้ฟ้า กลัวอะไรกับฝน."

Joom shifted to her knees and laughed. "You live under the sky." She laughed again. "You live under the sky. So, why are you afraid of the rain?"

"Yes." Nokyung flattened an area of sand. "Yes, that's what came into my head."

Far in the distance, a white boat sailed over the green water.

"Will you stay?"

She felt Joom's eyes fully on her.

"I will stay."

She searched among the bruises of Joom's face for the little sister of long ago. The one who ran squealing with her across the rice fields at night, fleeing from the ghosts that they imagined lurked in the shadows of the paddies. The ghosts were everywhere. You could not run fast enough.

A small crab, white, and all but translucent, scuttled briskly over a twist of rust-colored seaweed.

"He comes for us," Joom said, laughing.

They waved their fingers at the crab. It darted one way then the other and vanished inside a hole in the sand.

"He has gone home." Nokyung looked at Joom. "And you?"

"I am no crab," Joom said.

They rose from the sand, looked at each other, and heard a sound in the breeze coming off the Gulf. More than the whispering plash of the waves and the shrill cry of the sea birds, the sound had come from far away, had sought them, and had found them. A song from the north of Thailand. And they floated on its easy, melodic currents. It led them, as one figure, into the dance, and reminded them, as their fingers stretched long and curved in the warm air, their toes bent toward the polished blue sky, and their limbs waved with the graceful stalks of the sea oats, of what their grandmother had said about their lives.

A stick drawn through water.

Erik Heebner

The radio popped then softly crackled with the voice of a woman. Heebner noted that the address was in his area of responsibility. He requested backup and then turned the cruiser off the main highway into the glare of the afternoon sun and onto a long avenue toward the apartment complex. He lowered the visor to block the sun but the shafts of light were diffuse and easily penetrated his sunglasses. The warmth made him yawn, and his breath smelled of coffee; he drank as much as he could to stay awake. Double-duty was a mistake, and he wished he were in Enterprise with his wife and son.

Proceed with caution, dispatch said. A man, identified as Derrius Carter, a.k.a., SevenEight, had been shot and killed during the night and his body had been found next to Ray Reynold's cruiser. Reynolds was missing. An anonymous tip placed a man near the scene. The call had come from a cell phone belonging to Maria Castillo, an undocumented immigrant. The cottage where she'd been staying was cleaned out, abandoned. The phone had been found discarded in a restaurant bathroom east of the shooting site. A man matching the description of the suspect had been seen at the apartment complex.

Too much coffee, he was jittery, and the pounding glare of the sunlight, roasting him inside the uniform, dulled his senses. He reached for a sip from the thermos. The taste was cold and bitter, much like his life since the incident last year, but he was a good man, his wife said so, and with the help of a therapist, he'd come to believe it, or told himself that he believed it. The warehouse had been dark, the situation confusing, anyone could make a mistake. He had to let himself off the hook, his therapist said, and get back out there.

He was out now, and whatever confidence he had gained receded like a coward into the cave of his chest. All he had left was an inkling that it would show up when he needed it. Push on, he was told, and he listened, and the apartment complex—two grubby rooms and a bath—seemed to rise like a dilapidated mansion behind the gently flapping banners of a jet ski operation. The sun on the other side of the complex, he crossed through a gray, hazy shade into the lobby armed with a description of the suspect and the determination to play it right.

The clerk was certain the description matched the man in 113. Are you sure? Yes, he was sure. A large, brawny man, he said, and a woman was with him. A woman with a shaved head.

"With him?" He sought clarity from the clerk. Misinformation led to the warehouse confusion. "Together? Like a couple?"

"Hard to tell." Then the clerk's eyes widened. "She was beat up pretty bad, though."

"Did she appear coerced?"

The clerk shrugged.

"Are they still there?"

The clerk didn't know and gave him a passkey.

The setting sun cast a glow over the apartments, brilliantly lighting the buildings across the way, but he was on the shadowy side, where the light seemed to fizzle here and there in the blue shade and create illusion for the eyes. He felt oppressed by the cool, dim light and by the possibilities. A couple, most likely. And backup on the way. Watch and wait. That seemed prudent. But she'd been beaten up, the clerk said so, and even if it wasn't a hostage situation, the danger might be imminent. He went quietly and carefully along the breezeway, rehearsing procedure to make sure everything went right this time.

When he was near the door he unsnapped his sidearm, his hand light on the grip. Steady with the breath. Steady. He knocked. He called out. He waited. He began to hope that they had gone out. Yes, they had gone out, and backup would be along soon, and he relaxed. He then noticed his hand was sweaty and shaking. He read this as intuition, telling him they had not gone out, and that he must go in, and he slid the passkey into the slot.

A white beam of light lanced into the room, dividing it and casting a metallic sheen over the surfaces of a dented couch, a sagging lamp, and a skewed wall hanging. He recognized the print as a knock-off of Rembrandt's Lucretia. No one in this apartment complex could possibly understand the depth of emotion in the reproduction. Lucretia holds a rope taut in one hand and a dagger in the other. She has stabbed herself beneath the breast, and a streak of pale red blood stains her chemise. It feels unfinished, as if Rembrandt is still working on it, but the look is there. The resignation on Lucretia's shadowed face is unrelentingly gripping. He stood gazing at the painting and felt time crawl upon his skin, and the surroundings receded into slate-gray oblivion, and the man and the woman drifted in like shoddy phantoms, half-dressed, mouths slung open, from the shadows, and he was startled. His thumb snagged the holster, got caught in a panic, and the room expanded, large as the warehouse. The figures came toward him. A sharp pain in the knee, banged against the armrest of the couch, and a frantic hand preventing the fall. The woman cried out and the man rushed past her, in front of her. Looks of terror and chaos—and hope—in their faces, and the illumination from the crack in the curtain glinted off the metal at the end of the man's arm as it passed through the light into darkness. His thumb caught on the holster, his fingers seeking the grip, and they came fast, nearly on him, struggling, still struggling. He saw them, then past them, his wife and son in Enterprise, Lucretia on the wall, wronged by the hand of power, and his fingers closed on the grip and at last the gun came free.

Amnaj Boonngamanong

Amnaj fit the pry bar under the plywood and leveraged it off. Last one. All off and all stacked behind the building. A pine limb had snapped during the storm and now hung precariously over the roof of En La Playa. He wiped sweat from his brow.

"Just what I need," he said.

He collected the tools and looked again at the snapped limb. Didn't need to. But did. Something augural in its mangled form made a person look. Fate, and nothing else, would decide if it should fall.

He went to the front of the building. Blasko stood clean-shaven in old clothes.

"Storm wasn't that bad," Amnaj said. "Not bad enough to knock the scrag off your face. What happened?"

"Miss Jiiab," Blasko said. "I had no place to go, and she took me in. It was just awful. Made me bathe and . . . well, you see."

"She give you money?"

Blasko shook his head, a weary offer of the old sad-eye.

"Didn't think so," Amnaj said. "Not Jiiab." He opened the door. "Well, good seeing you. So long. No money, no beer. Best get on."

Blasko stuttered and coughed. "Well, thought. You know. After the storm and all. The first one might be free."

"You are one sad son of a bitch, Blasko." Amnaj reached

into his pocket and found what he thought was a receipt, wadded it into a tight ball, and threw it in Blasko's face. "Get out of here."

He went inside.

Blasko followed a moment later, unwadding the dollar bill that had hit him in the face. He walked straight to the bar and flattened the money on the counter. Nokyung, her shoulder trapping a phone to her ear, reached for the tap.

Amnaj shouted. "Tell him prices went up. Dollar and a quarter now."

He sat at a table next to Katia and laughed.

Blasko searched frantically through his pockets and landed a quarter. Held the quarter to his eye and moved it back and forth like a 3-D effect. Then he flipped a bird. Amnaj slapped the table and howled.

Katia was folding napkins. Her shape drew Amnaj in. Efficient and brown and terse. Fingers swift, and the long muscles rose and fell along her forearms and down the curved torso to the crossed legs beneath the table. He was about to speak when Nokyung, hanging up the phone, rushed over and sat down.

"Bright as a flower, isn't she?" Amnaj said to Katia. "If I could get that for the customers, I might make some money."

Katia, ignoring Amnaj, said, "What it is, Nokyung? Something good?"

"It is Joom and Jimmy Nails," she said. "They are together. She has just arrived at his apartment and slipped out to call me. If you heard her voice you would know that she is happy."

"I don't believe it," Amnaj said. "The way they go at each other."

"Uncle," Nokyung said. "It is like the sky after rain. A good thing in the world."

"Nothing in this world," he said, "is balance."

"No te creo, ¡qué ridículo!" Katia said. "You don't even make sense." She turned to Nokyung. "Don't listen to this heartless man." She scowled at Amnaj, her lip out, threatening. "¡Cállate and let them be happy," Katia said.

"I'll be happy if she doesn't quit the bar."

"A grump is what you are," Katia said. "Nokyung, tell Joom she should quit the bar. Soon as possible. Today, in fact. Tell her not to come in."

Then Katia resumed folding napkins, and Nokyung returned to the counter.

And long before he was aware of it, Amnaj once more found himself fascinated by the way Katia folded napkins in what he then realized was a kind of relentless dedication. She seemed unaware that he was admiring her work, the shape of her bending elbows, the caramel wash of her face, and then he thought of her as a lean animal in pursuit of prey. The image, yes, he liked it and smiled.

"How long you been with me?"

Katia paused, looked up.

"Seventeen years."

Her eyes, nearly black, fully round.

"That's a long time," he said.

"It's seventeen years," she said, turning flaps to rectangles.

"Did you know," then paused because she looked annoyed.

"Did you know my American wife married me for a cultural experience? Said my culture, my religion, might give her something that she'd lost in the hedonist capitalistic lifestyle of the typical American. Her experiment, that's what I was, that's what she said."

"I think you're a shit."

He smiled. A real gutsy woman.

"Well, there you go," he said. "Honest. It's a good start."

She turned the paper corners and leaned forward. The shirt, he saw, rose over a hip, and he imagined her bare back exposed.

"I was married once," she said.

"I know—"

"Idiota, you don't know." She rested her forearm on the table. "Not Reynolds. I mean somebody else."

She had his attention.

"His name was Camilo. He was a revolutionary, and true to his word, he died in a rebellion. And if the other faction had not killed him, then I would have, I was so angry. So, do you want to talk about marriage? To me? Do you?"

He took a stack and began to fold.

"Did I?"

"Well, fuck you did."

She sighed.

"I was sixteen years old, and do you know what I wanted?"

He ripped the fragile ends of the napkins and creased them quickly.

"I wanted someone to love."

Another stacked bundle filled his hands. He worked fast.

She reached out. "So, if that's not what you are talking about, then get away from me. And give me those napkins. You're doing them wrong."

The door swung open. Castro, his notebook clasped at his side.

"Quite a mess out there," Castro said.

Nokyung pried the lid off a Corona. She filled a glass with ice.

Amnaj rose. "Come in, come in."

"Are you open?"

Amnaj looked at Katia. She smiled and returned to the napkins.

"No storm's gonna close this bar."

He held the door for Castro and gestured to the seat at the counter, where the pale yellow drink, cool on the ice, waited for him.

Amnaj, half in, half out, looked at the dunes in the last light. The pier stood aslant like a giant caterpillar crawling out into the Gulf. Past it, the condos, like sheer cliffs darkened by cave entrances, overlooked the center of town and scattered below the walkways of motels and their rows of richly-colored aquamarine doors. Amnaj imagined the gold numbering above the peepholes of the rooms that housed the summer tourists. But they were gone now, having given up their leisure to flee the storm. And farther on, past Eileen's, the amusement park, normally lit up like a firework fountain, now in its mangled skeletal ruin, resembled a boneyard of prehistoric creatures. And beyond that the gray hump of the Seaside Bridge veered upward and out of sight like a road to the sky. Before them, as he shortened his view, the abandoned homes with sheared roofs, took on a filmy ghostly appearance and, though he knew they would again soon be occupied, he couldn't shake a feeling of disquiet as the late afternoon deepened into evening. And then he sharpened his focused on a fleet of approaching vehicles traveling with such urgency that waves of heat spread over the highway, and yet the convoy was so distant, it seemed as motionless as a column of ants on an impossible journey. But there was no mistaking who they were, as they rapidly advanced in close formation, their red and blue lights harshly striking the white canvas of the dunes and their high-pitched sirens, though muffled by distance, cutting the atmosphere like long sharp swords. And it was all too much to take in, and Amnaj turned away to the west, and as he turned, he felt behind him a presence, at his side, a familiar touch of fingers on his waist, but he didn't look back because he was drawn to the last warmth of the setting sun, where the pasty evening sky cast down blue shadows, and the sinter-green water quietly lapped the shore and—much farther out—the darkening horizon sloped beyond all sight.

"Do you see it on the hill?" Katia's hip pressed against him.

"What?"

"The statue of San Raphael, the shoulders, the head."

He held fast and let her hip work, her hand, a pointing finger, now in sight.

"An outline," he said. "It's all dark."

He could hear her breathing. A faint smell of garlic from her skin.

"It's still there," she said. "He's a healer, did you know? And a patron saint of travelers. I wonder if they're all right."

He turned, a fear gripped him. "Who?"

"Maria," she said, looking up, touching his arm. "Ray. Who did you think?"

He smiled. Then turned back to the sky. "They'll make it. Ray's smart, and Maria . . ."

"Maria's got balls."

Amnaj laughed. "Yes. Yes, she does."

"So did Camilo," she said. "And he wasn't wrong. But now he's dead."

The disquiet returned, always returned, squeezing. "Don't speak and wake him up," he said. "Let him stay in peace." He looked at the sign above En La Playa. He heard the sound of her foot scratching on the threshold.

"The last thing he did before going into the jungle was to bring me a bag of flour from the market."

Amnaj mumbled without opening his mouth. There was nothing to say. Night had fallen. And the first of the restored lights of Midsummer began to glisten like pearls on a bed of black velvet, and he picked them out, bleached lavender, graying blues, watery yellows. He pointed up. "Did you know the sign is bent?"

"I've known it for years."

"And you never said anything?"

"What's to say?"

She turned abruptly to go inside and as she turned he

swatted her bottom and expected her to swing back, look over her shoulder, raise a threatening fist, and laugh.

And that's exactly what she did.

ACKNOWLEDGMENTS

No one writes alone.

Thank you, Jonathan Starke, for the many long email exchanges in the shaping of this novel and for our explorations of the "gasp" moment. Janet Molino Garrett, Marta Cantwell, and Zoe Andrea Mason were so kind to help with the nuances of the Spanish language as it is spoken in Colombia and Mexico. Gracias.

Finally, I must thank Frank Green, mentor and friend, for his inspiration and commentary, and to his Bard Society for their invaluable critique and welcomed encouragement.

ABOUT THE AUTHOR

D. E. Lee's short fiction appears or is forthcoming in *Quiddity*, *Alligator Juniper*, *The Lindenwood Review*, *Saw Palm*, *Broad River Review*, and several other places. Awards include a Pushcart Prize nominaton, Finalist for *Nimrod's* 2011 Katherine Anne Porter Prize, Honorable Mention in *Glimmer Train's* 2014 Fiction Open, and Finalist for the 2014 Nelson Algren Award. *The Sky After Rain* was a Finalist for *Permafrost Magazine's* 2015 book prize and winner of the Brighthorse Prize for the Novel.